John M. Kingdom

Money

A Comedy, in Five Acts

John M. Kingdom

Money
A Comedy, in Five Acts

ISBN/EAN: 9783744788380

Printed in Europe, USA, Canada, Australia, Japan

Cover: Foto ©Andreas Hilbeck / pixelio.de

More available books at **www.hansebooks.com**

PRICE 15 CENTS.

DE WITT'S ACTING PLAYS.

(Number 184.)

MONEY.

A COMEDY,

IN FIVE ACTS.

BY LORD LYTTON,

(SIR EDWARD LYTTON BULWER.)

From the Original Text as first produced at the Theatre Royal, Haymarket, London, December 8, 1840, and at the Old Park Theatre, New York, Feb. 1, 1841.

AN ENTIRELY NEW ACTING EDITION.

With additional Stage Directions, accurately marked—Full Cast of Characters—Synopsis of Scenery—Costumes—Bill for Programmes—Story of the Play, and Remarks.

EDITED BY

JOHN M. KINGDOM,

Author of "*Marcoretti,*" "*The Fountain of Beauty,*" "*A Life's Vengeance,*"
"*Tancred,*" "*The High Road of Life,*" "*Which is My Husband!*"
"*The Old Ferry House,*" "*Madeline,*" "*Wreck of the Golden Mary,*" "*The Three Musketeers,*" *etc., etc.*

New-York:

ROBERT M. DE WITT, PUBLISHER,

No. 33 Rose Street.

 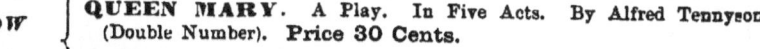

DE WITT'S HALF-DIME MUSIC

OF THE BEST SONGS FOR VOICE AND PIANO.

THIS SERIES of first class Songs contains th. Words and Music (with the Piano accompaniment of the most choice and exquisite Pieces, by the mos able, gifted and most popular composers. It contains every style of good Music—from the solemn and pathetic to the light and humorous. In brief, this collection is a complete Musical Library in itself, both of VOCAL *and* PIANO-FORTE MUSIC. *It is printed from new, clear, distinct, elegant Music Type, on fine white paper, made expressly for this Series, and is published at the low price of* FIVE CENTS.

Remember, EACH NUMBER CONTAINS A COMPLETE PIECE OF MUSIC, *beautifully printed on Sheet Music Paper.*

Any Twenty Pieces mailed on receipt of One Dollar, postage paid.

☞ *PLEASE ORDER BY THE NUMBERS.* ☜

Address,   **R. M. DE WITT, Publisher,**
33 Rose Street, N. Y.

SENTIMENTAL SONGS AND BALLADS.

MONEY.

A Comedy,

IN FIVE ACTS.

BY LORD LYTTON,
(SIR EDWARD LYTTON BULWER.)

FROM THE ORIGINAL TEXT AS FIRST PRODUCED AT THE THEATRE
ROYAL, HAYMARKET, LONDON, DEC. 8, 1840, AND AT THE OLD
PARK THEATRE, NEW YORK, FEB. 1, 1841.

AN ENTIRELY NEW ACTING EDITION.

WITH ADDITIONAL STAGE DIRECTIONS, ACCURATELY MARKED—FULL CAST
OF CHARACTERS—SYNOPSIS OF SCENERY—COSTUMES—
BILL FOR PROGRAMMES—STORY OF THE
PLAY AND REMARKS.

EDITED BY

JOHN M. KINGDOM,

*Author of "Marcoretti," "The Fountain of Beauty," "A Life's Vengeance," "Tancred,"
"The High Road of Life," "Which is My Husband?" "The Old Ferry
House," "Madeline," " Wreck of the Golden Mary,"
" The Three Musketeers," etc., etc.*

———◆———

NEW YORK:
ROBERT M. DE WITT, PUBLISHER,
No. 33 ROSE STREET.

(BETWEEN DUANE AND FRANKFORT STREETS.)

ORIGINAL CAST OF CHARACTERS.

	Theatre Royal, Haymarket, Dec. 8, 1840.	Old Park Theatre, New York, Feb. 1, 1841.
Alfred Evelyn	Mr. MACREADY.	Mr. HIELD.
Sir John Vesey	Mr. STRICKLAND.	Mr. CHIPPENDALE.
Lord Glossmore	Mr. F. VINING.	Mr. C. W. CLARKE.
Sir Frederick Blount	Mr. WALTER LACY	Mr. A. ANDERSON.
Benjamin Stout	Mr. D. REECE.	Mr. GUNN.
Graves	Mr. B. WEBSTER.	Mr. FISHER.
Captain Dudley Smooth	Mr. WRENCH.	Mr. NICKERSON.
Sharp	Mr. WALDRON.	Mr. BEDFORD.
Old Member	Mr. WILMOTT.	
Toke	Mr. OXBERRY.	
MacFinch	Mr. GOUGH.	
Crimson (a Portrait Painter)	Mr. GALLOT.	
MacStucco	Mr. MATTHEWS.	
Patent (a Coachmaker)	Mr. CLARKE.	
Frantz (a Tailor)	Mr. O. SMITH.	
Tabouret (an Upholsterer)	Mr. HOWE.	
Grab (a Publisher)	Mr. CAULFIELD.	
Clara Douglas	Miss H. FAUCIT.	Mrs. MAEDER.
Lady Franklin	Mrs. GLOVER.	Mrs. VERNON.
Georgina	Miss P. HORTON.	Mrs. CHIPPENDALE.

Officer, Club Members, Flat, Green, Waiters at Club, Pages, Servants.

TIME IN REPRESENTATION—THREE HOURS AND A HALF.

SCENERY.

ACT I.—Scene 1.—A Drawing-room in SIR JOHN VESEY'S house.

....Drawing-room beyond....

4th grooves.————........ | Folding doors. | ....————4th grooves.

A handsomely furnished, carpeted apartment. Folding doors open, showing another handsome room beyond. R. H., handsome table, upon which are newspapers, books, etc. L. H., another table, smaller, and near there a secretary writing-table, with a dozen chairs placed in the positions indicated.

ACT II.—Scene 1.—An Ante-room in EVELYN'S house. Small table R. H. Writing-desk and materials L. H. Chairs R. H and L. H. Door L. C. F.

Scene 2.—Drawing-room in SIR JOHN VESEY'S house, as before. Portfolio and drawings upon the side table.

ACT III.—Scene 1.—Drawing-room in SIR JOHN VESEY'S house, as before. The scene so arranged as to allow the next scene to close in.

Scene 2.—Boudoir in SIR JOHN VESEY'S house. The flats in the second groove represent a handsome apartment. Two chairs are brought on by the PAGE.

Scene 3.—Grand saloon at EVELYN'S club house.

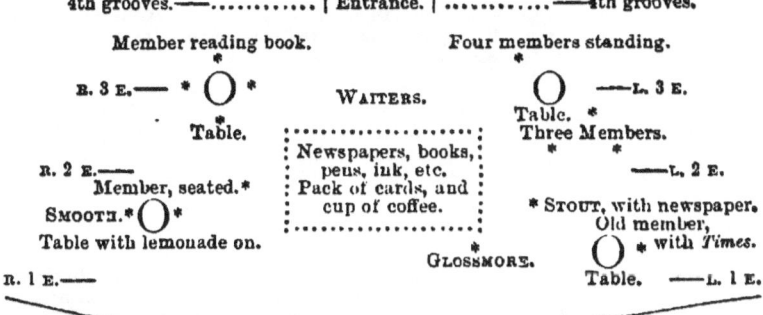

An elegantly furnished saloon with tables and chairs, and the other articles placed as shown in the diagram.

ACT IV.—Scene 1.—An ante-room in EVELYN'S, as before.

Scene 2.—A splendid saloon in EVELYN'S mansion.

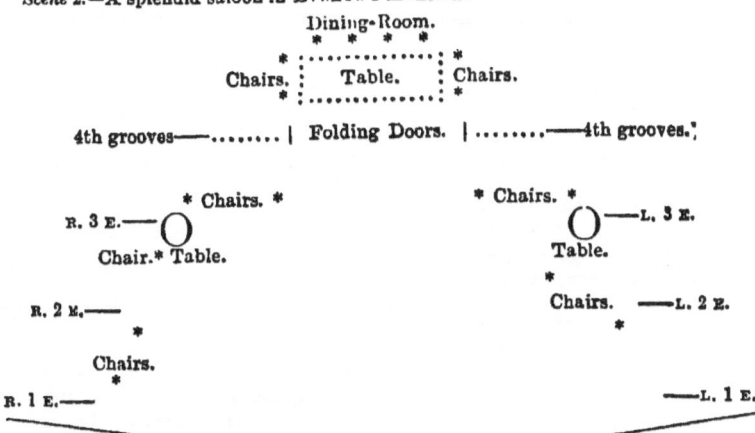

A magnificently furnished saloon, with paintings, etc. Two tables, R. H. and L. H., with candelabra. Chairs placed in the positions indicated. Folding doors C. F. Beyond them the interior of the dining-room, with chairs arranged for the guests— table spread for dinner. Candelabra, etc.

ACT V.—Scene 1.—Room at EVELYN'S club house. Handsomely furnished. Tables R. H. and L. H. Cloth and breakfast pieces on the table L. H. Doors C. F. Two chairs at each table. Papers, etc., on table R. H.

Scene 2.—Drawing-room in SIR JOHN VESEY'S house, as before.

Scene 3.—Saloon in EVELYN'S mansion, as before.

COSTUMES.

So far as the costumes of this play are concerned, there is nothing so very particular in the text, as in the previous plays, to rigidly compel an adherence to the one
style of the one particular period.

At the time the play was produced there was a very peculiar style of fashion prevailing in London. The Count D'Orsay was the leader, the model in fact. He was
at that time considered one of the most elegant and accomplished gentlemen; indeed, he might be termed the "Beau Brummell" of the period. It was the "D'Orsay hat," the "D'Orsay coat," the "D'Orsay vest," and "D'Orsay boots;" in fact,
everything in a fashionable West-end store bore the title.

As this play was originally played, the above style of costume was adopted; but
there is no actual necessity for it, and the costumes now given are expressly com-
piled for this edition of the work—observing a medium course between the past and
present; but they may be altered, according to the manager's views, to the leading
fashions prevailing at the time when the play is produced.

ALFRED EVELYN.—1st *Dress:* Frock coat and vest, black; dark trousers; black
necktie; boots. 2d *Dress:* Dark-blue frock coat; fancy mixture trousers and
vest; patent-leather boots; neck scarf; riding gloves and hat. In *Act IV.*, a
handsome dressing-gown, silk-lined, etc.; and then in *Scene* 2, black dress-coat,
white vest, black trousers, plain black necktie, patent-leather boots. *Act V.:*
The same, or a similar dress, to the one secondly described.

SIR JOHN VESEY.—Black dress-coat and trousers, white vest and cravat, pair of
gold-mounted eyeglasses, with black silk ribbon; hair white.

LORD GLOSSMORE.—Black frock coat and trousers, white vest, patent-leather boots,
scarf, and kid gloves. In *Act IV.*, usual dress for a fashionable dinner-party.

SIR FREDERICK BLOUNT.—In the 1st *Act*, a plain black suit—handsome garments of
any color, but made in the highest fashion and of the very best quality—rich
silk handkerchiefs, and very fine light-colored overcoat, etc.*

STOUT.—Blue cloth coat with broad tails; velvet vest, white cravat, and stand-up
collar; Oxford gray trousers, cloth boots, large red handkerchief, white hat
with black band, afterwards removed.

GRAVES.—Body coat, vest, trousers, and gloves all black. In *Act III.*, a colored
silk handkerchief.

CAPTAIN DUDLEY SMOOTH.—1st *Dress:* Dark fashionable morning or lounging coat,
vest, and trousers. 2d *Dress:* Frock coat and fancy colored vest and trousers,
patent-leather boots. 3d *Dress:* Usual dress for a fashionable dinner-party.

SHARP.—Plain black body coat, vest, and trousers; white cravat, shoes.

OLD MEMBER.—Blue colored body coat with gilt buttons, fancy colored vest, nan-
keen trousers, shoes and cloth gaiters, white scarf, and high collar.

CLARA DOUGLAS.—1st *Dress:* Plain black walking dress with sleeves, and the hair
plain. 2d *Dress:* Fancy muslin dress, ornamented, but not too much, accom-
panied by rich gold bracelets, etc. 3d *Dress:* A rich dark velvet walking costume, and handsome ornaments.

LADY FRANKLIN.—A very rich and gay colored silk dress, with lace shawl, etc. In
Act IV., handsome evening dress, the sleeves being short. In *Act V.*, a handsome morning costume, bonnet and lace shawl.

GEORGINA.—White muslin dress trimmed fancifully with black ribbons, jet ornaments on the breast and the wrists of the long sleeves; neck-chain of jet. In
Act II., similar dress varied by fancy ribbons and gold ornaments. In *Act IV.*,
change for dress for a fashionable dinner-party. In *Act V.*, silk dress, fashion-
ably cut blue mantle and trimmings; hat and feather.

SERVANTS.—Those belonging to SIR JOHN VESEY and ALFRED EVELYN: Plain black
body coat, vest, and knee-breeches, white stockings and shoes. Those at the
Club House: Puce colored body coats, with large brass buttons, velvet plush
vests and knee-breeches, white neckties and stockings, shoes, and hair powdered.

---

* All actors whom I have seen play this part made it the medium for the display
of the richest and most fashionable clothing.

PROPERTIES.

ACT I., Scene 1.—Two rich tables and covers; newspapers, books; twelve chairs; carpet; a secretaire writing table; writing materials; black-edged letter; watch; purse; banknote; wine; decanters; glasses; cake; will; letter;

ACT II., Scene 1.—Three drawings; bundle with new coat; writing desk and materials; table; chairs: book and parchment; piece of gold coin; letter. *Scene* 2.—As in Act I., with the addition of portfolio, drawings; a portrait; letter, as in last.

ACT III., Scene 1.—Same furniture, etc., as in Act I., Scene 1, except there need not be so many chairs; writing materials; letter. *Scene* 2.—Two chairs. *Scene* 3.—Five tables; twelve chairs; newspapers; books; writing materials; playing cards; coffee cups; large round snuff-box; two salvers; glasses; letter; note; pocket-book; wax lights in candelabras on the tables; lemonade and glasses.

ACT IV., Scene 1.—Two tables; two chairs; writing materials; pocket-book; checks. *Scene* 2.—Two tables with candelabra, etc.; nine chairs; painting; letter; paper for Sheriff's officer; table in dining-room at back; chairs round it; dinner service spread; candelabra and lights.

ACT V., Scene 1.—Two tables; four chairs; table cloth and breakfast things; glasses and wine; letter; bill; salver; large and shall watches. *Scene* 2.—Bell pull and bell without. *Scene* 3.—Same as Act IV., Scene 2. Letter, salver, writing materials on table.

EXPLANATION OF THE STAGE DIRECTIONS.

The Actor is supposed to face the Audience.

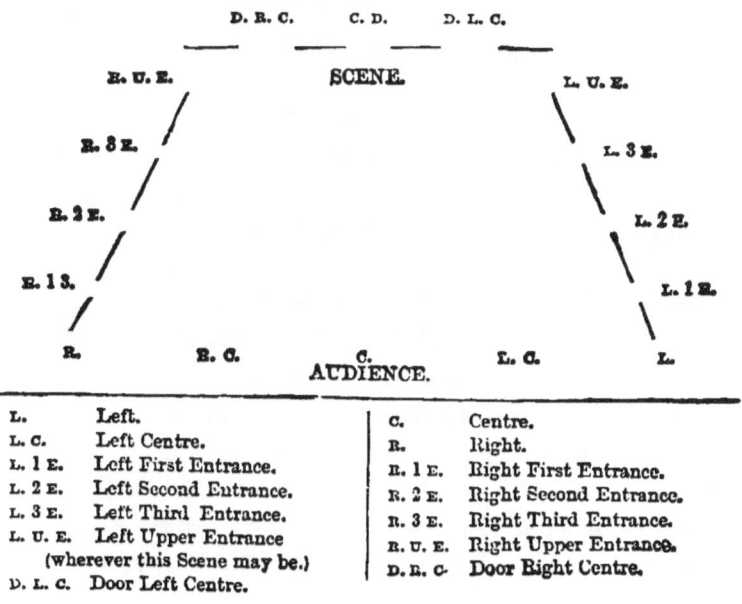

L.	Left.	c.	Centre.
L. C.	Left Centre.	R.	Right.
L. 1 E.	Left First Entrance.	R. 1 E.	Right First Entrance.
L. 2 E.	Left Second Entrance.	R. 2 E.	Right Second Entrance.
L. 3 E.	Left Third Entrance.	R. 3 E.	Right Third Entrance.
L. U. E.	Left Upper Entrance	R. U. E.	Right Upper Entrance.
	(wherever this Scene may be.)	D. R. C	Door Right Centre.
D. L. C.	Door Left Centre.		

BILL FOR PROGRAMMES, *Etc.*

The events of this play take place in London.   Period, the present century.

ACT I.

SCENE I.—DRAWING-ROOM IN SIR JOHN VESEY'S HOUSE.

*The Scheming Baronet and his Daughter—Death of a Rich Indian Cousin
—The Poor Secretary and the Poor Ward—The Story of Evelyn's Love
—Offer of Hand and Heart—Clara's Rejection—A Tale of Sorrow—
The Reading of the Will—"I leave all the residue of my fortune to
——Alfred Evelyn."*

———

ACT II.

SCENE I.—AN ANTE-ROOM IN EVELYN'S NEW MANSION.

*The Troubles of Riches – Specimen of a Political Economist—Election
Prospects—Bribery and Corruption—A Game of Battledore and Shuttle-
cock—The Story of Evelyn's Life and Struggles—The Mysterious Letter—" Who sent it ?   Clara or Georgina ? "*

SCENE II.—DRAWING-ROOM AT SIR JOHN VESEY'S.

*Mr. Graves and his " Sainted Maria "—A Dangerous Widow—The Baronet's
Cunning—An Artful Trick to Entrap Evelyn—The Portait—The Bait
Caught—The Letter was from Georgina—She Sent her Savings to Re-
lieve Distress—The Offer of Hand and Fortune to Georgina—Evelyn is
Accepted—Clara's Agony—" With my whole heart I say it—be happy ! "*

———

ACT III.

SCENE I.—DRAWING-ROOMS IN SIR JOHN VESEY'S HOUSE.

*Clouds in the Horizon—Extravagance and Gambling—Rocks Ahead—Clara's
Departure from England—The Warning Voice of Love, as a Sister—
" Let us part friends ! " — Suspicions of Truth—Graves' Story of
Georgina's Flirtations—A Trap Set for the Trapper.*

SCENE II.—BOUDOIR IN SIR JOHN VESEY'S HOUSE.

*A Widower and Widow in Love—The Temptations of a Charming Woman
—A Cure for Melancholy—Dancing and a Sweet Voice—Unpleasant
Interruption.*

SCENE III.—GRAND SALOON AT EVELYN'S CLUB HOUSE.

*A Gentleman and a Gambler—Captain DEADLY Smooth's Good Luck—Plot
and Counterplot—Infatuation in Gaming—Loss after Loss—Evelyn's
Ruin Approaching.*

ACT IV.

Scene I.—ANTE-ROOM IN EVELYN'S HOUSE.

*Morning Calls—Debt Against Debt—Novel Mode of Payment by Increasing
—Not Quite Sharp Enough.*

Scene II.—SPLENDID SALOON IN EVELYN'S HOUSE.

*The Plot Thickens—Evelyn is Drifting Wrong—Suggestions for Assist-
ance—" Will Georgina help me?—£10,000 for a time will save me "
—An Answer Deferred—Unpleasant Duns and a Sherriff's Officer—
Failure of Evelyn's Bankers—Clamorous Creditors—Pleasure
Against Charity—Desertion of Friends as the Money goes Down!*

———

ACT V.

Scene I.—A ROOM AT THE CLUB.

*More News of the Downfall—A Friend in the Scheme—Georgina's Old Love
—The Eccentric Baronet—Political Intrigues—The Mine is Opening.*

Scene II.—DRAWING-ROOMS IN SIR JOHN VESEY'S HOUSE.

*A Devoted Heart—A Woman in Distress—The Old Love Revived—If he
Can be Saved he Shall—Departure of Clara to see Evelyn.*

Scene III.—SPLENDID SALOON IN EVELYN'S HOUSE.

*Money Works Wonders—A Change from Respect to Infamy—'Tis the
way of the World—£10,000 placed at Evelyn's Bankers—Saved—
" 'Tis Georgina's act—the die is cast!"—Lovers Alone—The Story
of Clara's Life—The Reasons for Rejection—Hope for the Future—
Too Late!—Evelyn Elected a Member of Parliament—The Mine is
Sprung—Startling News—Georgina Marries Sir Frederick Blount!
" Who, then, sent the money to my bankers?"—The Mystery Solved
—The Letter Explained—Clara Douglas!—Acceptance of Evelyn
—The Scheme at an End—He was Never Ruined—Only a Plot to
Show the Value of*

MONEY.

THE STORY OF THE PLAY.

IN the centre of the most fashionable part of London there resided, at the commencement of the play, Sir John Vesey, Baronet, ex-Member of Parliament, etc., Fellow of ever so many societies, and President of ever so many Corporations; in fact, a man surrounded by all the attributes of wealth and high political and social position. Outwardly well polished, he had naturally a large and influential circle of admiring friends and cringing flatterers; wealth and position, like honey, attract many flies—and an artifice he resorted to of getting it mooted about that he was hoarding up his money, gradually acquired him the name of "Stingy Jack," and stimulated a belief, in some persons, and confirmed the opinion of others, that he really was a most highly honorable and wealthy gentleman, though somewhat eccentric, and that his only daughter, Georgina, was a rich heiress.

The fact, however, was just the reverse. He had been, and was, playing a very deep game indeed; he was in every respect an unprincipled and unsubstantial man, —a living specimen, though more advanced in years, of Dickens' ever to be remembered character, Montague Tigg, *alias* Tigg Montague.

The members of Sir John Vesey's household were Georgina, his daughter; Lady Franklin, his half-sister and a widow; Clara Douglas, a poor orphan cousin and his ward, and Alfred Evelyn, another poor cousin, who acted as his private secretary.

As to Sir John himself—his father for services rendered in the army obtained a title, but expended all available means in keeping it up, consequently the only fortune he could leave his son was the title. But this worthy son was not to be so easily foiled. On the strength of his parent's services, he obtained a pension of £400 a pear, which was quite sufficient trading capital for a man of Sir John's adventurous disposition and tactics. On £400 he took credit for £800; upon which credit he married a woman with £10,000, and increased his credit to £40,000. Then it was that he worked his artful scheme and paid a highly respectable but impoverished gentleman so much per week to mix in society and constantly allude to him as "Stingy Jack," upon the principle that if a man of position is called "stingy" he is presumed to be "rich," and to be presumed "rich," is to be universally respected.

Working the wires thus, he had been elected a member of Parliament, and remained so until a fitting opportunity arrived, when he resigned his seat in favor of a member of the Government, who, in return, gave him a sinecure appointment, bringing in about £2,000 a year; all of which, and more raised upon the strength of it, he expended annually in keeping up appearances, in the hopes of bringing about a wealthy match for his daughter.

Of Georgina little can be said, except that she was quite obedient to her father's wishes, though at the same time a little artful and self-willed. Her mother died young, and therefore the male parental guidance had its effect in moulding her to his views.

Lady Franklin was generous, kind, wealthy, and middled-aged—without any family, and therefore her half-brother had induced her to take off his hands the burden of his ward. Clara Douglas was an orphan of his cousin; her mother died young, and her father at his death left her to the care of Sir John as her guardian, but having no wealth, that was all he did leave him, and therefore to a man of Sir John's temperament it was by no means an agreeable bequest. It was not long, however, before he found a way to transfer the charge to Lady Franklin.

Alfred Evelyn was left fatherless when a boy and his mother sacrificed everything she could to give him education. From school he proceeded to college, where he became a "sizar."*

---

* "Sizar" is a term used in the University of Cambridge, in England, to denote a body of students, next below the pensioners, who eat at the public table free of expense, after the fellows of the college have taken their meals. In former times they had to wait at table during the meal hours, but this custom has been done

One day, a young lord struck him, he returned the insult by horsewhipping his assailant. The then great difference between rich and poor was too strong for the affair to be passed over, so poor Evelyn was expelled the college and all his ambitious hopes blasted. Coming to London, he toiled and toiled to the best of his ability to earn a scanty subsistence for himself and mother, and so long as she lived he labored strenuously and successfully, but with her death, ambition seemed to expire also. As a last resource, he consented to become the ill-paid secretary and hanger-on to his cousin, Sir John Vesey; but there was a magnet in the house which attracted him; he loved Clara Douglas, and to be near that loadstone he sank his pride.

He prepared Sir John's speeches, wrote his pamphlets, made up his calculations, composed epitaphs, condensed the debates in Parliament, and even executed various orders for the ladies, in bringing home dresses, novels, music, securing boxes at the opera, etc.,—all done probably upon a salary less than was paid to Sir John's coachman. Such, then, were the constituent elements of the Baronet's household at the opening of the play.

Sir John has just received a letter from Mr. Graves, an eccentric, but well-meaning middle-aged gentleman, who never ceases to express, with a melancholy air, the loss he experienced by the death of his late wife; whom he invariably terms, with uplifted eyes, his "Sainted Maria," though very probably, if the truth were known, she had led him anything but a happy life, and her departure from this world was more of a blessing than a misfortune; at least, so many persons said, and more believed.

Mr. Graves informs Sir John that a Mr. Mordaunt, to whom Georgina is the nearest relation, is dead; that, having been appointed executor, and having since his wife's death lived only in apartments, he proposes to read the will that day at Sir John's house, and will come with Mr. Sharp, the lawyer, for that purpose.

This is great news to Sir John—Mr. Mordaunt was reputed to be worth half a million sterling; Georgina is the nearest relation—there could surely be nothing therefore to prevent her coming in for the bulk of his fortune.

Lady Franklin and Clara arrive; to the surprise of the worldly-minded Sir John, his half sister is not in mourning, but poor Clara is, explaining in the genuine feeling of her nature, that although only a third cousin of the deceased, he had once assisted her father, and the quiet mourning robes she had obtained were all the respect and gratitude she could show.

There are other distant relatives interested in the will; Mr. Stout, a political economist, Lord Glossmore, a sort of butterfly nobleman: and Sir Frederick Blount, a foppish baronet, who, as Lady Franklin facetiously observes, "objects to the letter r as being too wough and therefore dwops its acquaintance."

Alfred Evelyn, in the meantime, has arrived, and sits at the table absorbed in reading; so, when the conversation flags, a general attack is made upon him to know if he has executed various commissions, and what has delayed him. He takes the opportunity to explain to Sir John, that his prolonged absence has been occasioned by his having gone to visit a poor woman who was his nurse, and his mother's last friend; that she is very sick, nay, dying, that she owes six months rent, and he appeals to Sir John for assistance. It is refused; but Georgina overhears it, and her first impulse is to assist him, but then she might not have the fortune, her allowance is very little, and she *must* purchase a pair of earrings she has seen; she, however, inquires the address of the nurse. Upon this point the play hinges. Evelyn is misled by her unsolicited generosity, and gives it, and as Georgina reads it aloud, Clara silently takes a note of it, places all her little money in an envelope—but how to direct it? Evelyn would know her handwriting, and that must not be, so she appeals to Lady Franklin, who promises that he shall not know

---

away with some years. The term so applied to them was probably derived from this ancient occupation, as the food they had to supply when so engaged was called "size." It may well be imagined how naturally a spirit like Evelyn's recoiled at the position.

it, that her ward shall direct it, and she will herself furnish the money, as it is more than Clara can spare.

Sir Frederick Blount arrives, and in his stupid, foppish way, addresses many very ridiculous observations to Clara, which produces some excellent by-play and sarcastic remarks from Evelyn, who, though apparently sitting at the table reading, is watching with a keen and jealous eye every movement of the idol of his affections. Sir Frederick being called away, they are left alone, and in the most exquisite and perfect language, he tells the story of his love. But what is his horror and dismay to meet a calm, yet firm, refusal! Clara sees that, poor as they are, it would only be a marriage of privation and of penury—a life of days that dread the morrow—her love is his—she can submit to suffer alone, but bring him into it also, she cannot.

Mr. Graves and Mr. Sharp the lawyer arrive, and the reading of the will commences. Much disappointment, but more amusement, is created by the peculiarity and smallness of the bequests ; the largest being one of £10,000 to Georgina Vesey.

" What can the old fool have done with his money !" exclaims Sir John, losing all control. The climax soon comes; the deceased bequeaths the entire residue of his immense fortune to the only relative who never fawned upon him, and who, having known privation, may the better employ wealth—Alfred Evelyn ! Congratulations on every side are unbounded, but the voice of her he loves is silent.

Evelyn is speedily installed in the first style of position ; his patronage is sought by every one ; tradesmen, electors, artists, and every rank of persons—but this does not prevent his dispensing charity with a liberal hand, for which he secures the services of Mr. Sharp.

To Graves he tells the story of his life and love, and further, that in the letter which the lawyer gave him after the reading of the will, there was a request from Mr. Mordaunt—but not imposing any condition—asking as a favor, if he had formed no other attachment, to choose as his wife, either Georgina or Clara, who was the daughter of a dear friend of the deceased. He still loves Clara, but her rejection overcomes him ; besides, he has obtained the letter, written in a disguised hand, sending money to, and saving his nurse. His heart yearns to believe that it was Clara's doing, but he cannot conceive how she should know the address, besides the amount was too much for her to send. He also tells Graves, that determined to be revenged upon Clara for refusing him, he has bribed Sharp, the lawyer, to say that the letter he gave him contained a codicil to the will, bequeathing Clara £20,000 ; so that she will be no longer a dependent, and that she will owe her release from almost beggary and insult, unknowingly, to the poor scholar whom she had rejected. With this joyous and noble feeling he determines to visit Lady Franklin, and see if he can possibly ascertain by whom the money was sent to his nurse.

Consequent upon her unlooked-for wealth, Clara is now admired by all, even by Sir Frederick. Lady Franklin always assures her she believes Evelyn still loves her, and begs permission to tell him who sent the money to the nurse, otherwise he might imagine it came from Georgina. Sir John Vesey happens to overhear this remark, and determines to improve upon it, to secure Evelyn for his daughter. Clara makes Lady Franklin promise never to reveal the secret—most reluctantly she obeys.

Sir John questions his daughter ; she had taken down the address, intending to, but did not, send the money. That is quite enough ground for Sir John to work upon.

A new character now comes upon the scene, Captain Dudley Smooth, but who, in consequence of his fashionable manners and abilities, unusual success at the gaming table, and skill as a duellist, had acquired the name of " Deadly " Smooth, and he is of course soon one of the friends of the wealthy Evelyn.

Sir Frederick Blount also seeks Evelyn's aid to promote his suit with Clara, telling him that he finds Georgina had a prior attachment, which prior attachment was no other than Evelyn himself, and therefore he must give her up and try his luck with Clara. Evelyn agrees to help him, and urges his merits in a bantering tone. Observing Sir Frederick's attentions, Georgina determines to flirt with Evelyn, and

Sir John seizes the opportunity to introduce to his notice a portfolio of her drawings; turning them over one after another until up comes a portrait of—Alfred Evelyn!

He is astonished and confused. Can she really love him? A thought strikes 'im—carelessly he asks her if she has yet purchased a guitar she spoke of some months since. Now is the time for the master stroke, so taking him aside, Sir John hints that she had applied the money in charity; that she did not wish it known, and had employed some one else to direct the letter. The blow is well struck, the shaft strikes home; such benevolence, and such love as to draw his portrait ; Clara had refused him, how could he do otherwise than offer to Georgina? He frankly tells her of his love for another, deep and true, but *vain*, that he cannot give her a first love, but he does offer her esteem, gratitude, hand and fortune.

It is accepted. Poor Clara overhears all, and sinks on her chair fainting; he rushes to her side, and she rallies sufficiently to exclaim, " With my whole heart I say it—be happy—Alfred Evelyn !"

The time for the wedding is somewhat delayed, much to Sir John's annoyance, and Georgina complains that Evelyn's visits are not so frequent, nor his manners so cheerful as they used to be—indeed, her former admirer, Sir Frederick, was far more attentive and amusing. Sir John does not half like the way Evelyn is going on. Fine houses in London, and in the country balls, banquets, expensive pictures, horses, liberal charities, everything tending to diminish rapidly the largest fortune. In addition to which, it is reported, he has taken to gambling, and is nearly always in company with Captain *Deadly* Smooth, against whose arts, no young man of fortune had been known to stand long.

Sir John determines that it is absolutely necessary to bring about an early settlement, and to further this, he thinks it best to get Clara away. He speaks to her upon the subject, and she consents to leave England rather than cloud his daughter's hopes, and to that effect promises to write a letter. As she is finishing it, Evelyn calls to see Georgina, who is out, and, as they are alone, Clara tells him of her intended departure.

In a scene of the most choice and beautiful language, replete with exquisite pathos, she breathes her thanks for past kindness, and now, that he is betrothed to another, her love—as a sister—dictates to her to remonstrate with him upon his parade, and luxuries, and follies. But he tells her that this casting aside of his high qualities, this dalliance with a loftier fate, was her own work. It is impossible adequately to describe the pure and beautiful language of this scene—the skillful mingling of love and reproaches—and the bitter parting—as friends!

As he is recovering from the blow, Graves meets him, and tells him that he knows for a fact, Sir Frederick has proposed to Clara and been refused ; nay, more, that Georgina is not in love with him, but only with his fortune ; and that she plays affection with him in the afternoon, after she has practiced with Sir Frederick in the morning. And further, that Sir John is vastly alarmed at his gambling propensities, and his connection with Captain Smooth, so much so, that he intends visiting the club that evening to watch him.

A light breaks upon Evelyn, and he assures Graves that if these stories are true, the duper shall be duped, and he will extricate himself; to this end, he determines to shape his plans.

One of the liveliest scenes in the play here follows between Lady Franklin, who is really in love with the solemn and melancholy Graves. She so talks and works upon his feelings, that he gradually relaxes his staid demeanor, and actually joins her in a dance, her own sweet, merry voice supplying the music. In the midst of their meriment they are interrupted and confused by the sudden entrance of Sir John, Blount and Georgina. It is the finest piece of comedy ever put upon the stage, and affords scope for excellent acting.

We are now introduced to the club. Evelyn arrives, and requests Smooth to play with him, and he loses game after game. Watching his opportunity, he takes the Captain aside and acquaints him with a plot he has formed to test the truth of his suspicions of the intentions of Georgina and her father—into this scheme, Smooth readily enters, and returning to the table, they renew their play. Sir John arrives, and watches with the most intense excitement, game after game lost, with constantly increasing stakes. In apparent agony, Evelyn rises from the table, declaring that the work is ruinous, and he will play no more. All the members crowd round the Captain to ascertain the extent of his winnings; the only answer they get is an offer to purchase from one of them a furnished house which he has to sell for £15,000, which, from his manner, he leads them to believe, is a mere trifle. They catch the bait, and at once imagine he must have won double and treble that sum. Sir John's consternation is fearful, but the more so when he sees Evelyn, apparently under the influence of too much wine, take hold of Smooth's arm, and declare they must now make a night of it.

In the morning, Glossmore and Sir Frederick call upon Evelyn to settle some small accounts with him. He still carries on the deception, and not only excuses paying them, but works a trick between them, by which he secures a further check from each, and makes a present to one of a horse he buys on credit from the other. He goes further than this; not only does he borrow £500 from Sir John, but he also tells him that he has sold out of the funds sufficient money to pay the balance for the purchase of an estate; that the money is laying at his bankers, but he cannot touch it for any other purpose, or the estate will be lost, and the deposit money he has paid forefeited. He alludes, therefore, to Georgina's £10,000 legacy, and managing cleverly to get Sir John out of the way, he speaks to her upon the subject. He tells her of his position, that they may probably have to retrench and live in the country, and suggests that she should lend him the £10,000 for a few weeks to meet some pressing claims; without confidence there can be no joy in wedlock. She hesitates, then promises he shall hear from her.

Smooth, Glossmore and others now arrive, and, still carrying on the deception, he appears most servile and cringing to the Captain. In a well constructed scene, he calls the attention of all to his unexpected accession to wealth twelve months since, and claims their good opinion for the way in which he has acted—they all outwardly approve, but inwardly they earnestly wish they had back their various loans. Their nervous excitement is increased by news being brought that the bankers with whom he banked have suspended payment, and they very much doubt his assurance that he had not much money there. This is followed by several tradesmen applying for their bills, and then by the entry of a sheriff's officer to serve him with a summons. All this is too overpowering—Sir John vehemently demands his £500, and the others join chorus. Graves is overcome; he tells Evelyn to go into dinner, and he will settle with the officer. Delighted at this generosity, Lady Franklin ingenuously exclaims, "I love you for that!" and poor Graves loses his usual solemnity in the pleasure he experiences at this avowal.

Again Evelyn appeals to Georgina; he shall hear to-morrow; but Sir John can restrain himself no longer, and he commands her, as his "poor, injured, innocent child," to take the arm of Sir Frederick Blount. The doors are thrown open, and Evelyn invites all his friends to the dinner prepared for them; but in doing so, he appeals to them, in mockery, to lend him £10 for his poor old nurse. This is too much, and he then bitterly reminds them that in the morning they lent him hundreds for pleasure, but now they refuse him a trifle for charity, and he commands them to go. Smooth alone remains, and being joined by Graves, the three repair to the table " to fill a bumper to the brave hearts that never desert us!"

Events now approach a climax. Graves and Lady Franklin have become more intimate and confidential. He tells her he is certain that Evelyn still loves Clara, but doubts if she cares for him. Lady Franklin, on the other hand, assures him that ever since she has heard of Evelyn's distress, she has been breaking her heart for him.

Clara arrives, having been to her bankers, for what purpose she declines to say; but she says she has heard that £10,000 would relieve Evelyn, and probably Georgina would lend him the amount. Graves much doubts such generosity in a woman, but he hints that he knew of greater generosity in a man, who, rejected in poverty, by one as poor as himself, when he became rich, through a well invented codicil, had made the woman rich. A light dawns upon Clara, she will see Evelyn and know the truth.

Evelyn's scheme has thus far succeeded. Upon Graves offering to aid him all he can, he is so pleased that he reveals his true position, and assures him that scarcely a month's income of his large fortune has been touched; it was merely a ruse to see whether a woman's love was given to " man " or " money." If Georgina should prove by her answer her confidence and generosity, then, though his heart should break, he would marry her ; on the other hand, should she decline, there would be hope for explanations with Clara.

A letter is brought in, and upon opening it, he finds a notice that £10,000 has been paid into the bank to his account. This decides the matter—the die is cast, and Georgina wins. Lady Franklin arrives with Clara, and compelling Graves to withdraw, leaves her and Evelyn together.

In brilliant and telling language, the true and noble sentiments of Clara are revealed ; explanation upon explanation follows, and the ardent love of both is powerfully and touchingly portrayed ; but it is too late ! Evelyn, still believing that it is Georgina who has assisted him, asserts, that by every tie of faith, gratitude, loyalty and love, he is bound to another ! Sir John hurries in, stating that he has an offer from Georgina to advance the money, and is astounded when Evelyn tells him the amount has been already paid into his bankers. Then Sharp arrives with the news that Evelyn has been elected a Member of Parliament, and he also informs Sir John that the loss by the failure of the bank was only £200 or so, and that Evelyn has always been living within his income. This is indeed good news, and Sir John is in ecstacies, when his daughter and Sir Frederick arrive ; but before he can speak, Evelyn addresses her, desiring to know if she has assisted and trusted him purely and sincerely. She cannot comprehend him, and tells him, that following the principles she once heard uttered, " what is money without happiness ?" she had, that morning, promised her hand to Sir Frederick Blount ! Utterly astounded, Evelyn produces the letter—Lady Franklin reads it—the money had been paid in by " a friend, to Alfred Evelyn ;" the same name used in sending the money to the old nurse, and she at once proclaims both as Clara's acts. In an ecstacy of delight, Evelyn offers love and fortune ; *this* time he is not rejected. The solemn Graves forgets his " sainted Maria," and joins hands with Lady Franklin, and all but Sir John realize the combination of happiness and—MONEY !

REMARKS.

IN introducing the third, in the new series of Bulwer's plays, it is a labor of love. The recollections of its excellent production, and of witnessing it afterwards upon almost every occasion of its reproduction in London, bring to mind old associations that are agreeable, yet saddening ; for many of those who filled the parts, and whose company was ever welcome, both on and off the stage, are now no more.

Of all Bulwer's plays, this is, undoubtedly the best—it is more than fine—it is a splendid comedy, so telling, and so true to life in all the principles, and in the delineation of characters with which a wayfarer through the world constantly meets. It makes such a powerful appeal, in presenting the spectacle of a man endowed with intellect, education, and gentlemanly bearing, occupying a subordinate position, but expected to be of the greatest usefulness upon all occasions, at the same time receiving less pay than the tall footman of the establishment, and considerable fewer perquisites than the favorite butler ; a position from which he is only released by a most unexpected stroke of fortune.

The conception and the execution of the plot are, in my opinion, perfect. All the observations touching upon falsity, pride, deceptive appearances, worldly scheming, pure affection, hypocrisy, are painted and well drawn, so admirably depictured, that they cannot fail to tell.

Upon reference to the remarks and dates in the previous plays, it will be found that only about eleven months elapsed between the production of the Lady of Lyons and Richelieu, whereas, between that play and this, nearly double that period passed away, and certain it is, that the author made good use of it, by producing a work, both in plot and language, very far surpassing all his previous efforts, and giving to the world one of the finest comedies, if not *the* finest, in the English language.

He had again the good luck to be supported by the highest professional material available for carrying out his ideas, and it can be stated, from personal knowledge of all the ladies and gentlemen engaged in the play, that the characters were well suited to the actors, and the actors to the characters; consequently, nothing could be more felicitous or so likely to ensure success, as the result proved. Again he had for his hero, Alfred Evelyn, Mr. Macready, the hero of his previous plays, and for his heroine, Clara Douglas, Miss Helen Faucit, who had contributed so largely to previous successes.

As was noticed in the remarks to the Lady of Lyons and Richelieu, those plays had the benefit of being supported by actors, all of whom afterwards attained leading positions in the profession; so was it with this play. On its first production there was a concentration of talent, blooming, half blooming, and about to bloom, that ensured a proper rendering of a meritorious play.

It will be observed, that the scene of triumph was changed from the Theatre Royal, Covent Garden, to the Theatre Royal, Haymarket, London; and that of the ladies and gentlemen who had played in the author's previous productions, only four had parts in this, viz: Miss H. Faucit, Mr. Macready, Mr. F. Vining, and Mr. Howe. But the others were a little host. Mr. Walter Lacy, one of the finest, and most gentlemanly actors on the stage; Mr. B. Webster, a great actor, and for many years lessee of the Haymarket, Adelphi, and Princess' Theatres, in London, where he is still playing, at an advanced age, and who is celebrated for having brought out, at the Adelphi Theatre, in conjunction with Madame Celeste, a very large number of first class dramas—" The Hop Pickers,"—" The Harvest Home," —" The Green Bushes," and farces innumerable. Mr. Wrench and Mr. Oxberry, low comedians of the first class; the latter, a gentleman of much intellect and education, as his " Dramatic Budget " will testify.

Mr. O. Smith, who for many years played the " villain " in all domestic dramas, with unqualified success, so good was his make up, and so well adapted for such character, his cool, deep voice. Mrs. Glover, a most amiable and accomplished lady, who was for many years a stock member of the Haymarket Company, and as famous in London, for her admirable delineation of ladies of middle and more advanced age, as Mrs. Wheately was in this country. Lastly, Miss P. Horton, who was afterwards, for many years without a rival, as the chief burlesque and extravaganza actress in London. She married Mr. T. G Reed, a celebrated musical director and composer, and together they carried on for many years a beautiful little theatre in Regent street, London, where they produced a number of musical pieces of the highest class; it was like a handsome drawing-room, and was known as " The Gallery of Illustration."

Poor Mrs. Glover met with a melancholy end. Upon the occasion of her farewell benefit in London, July 12th, 1850, she was so overcome by the reception given to her, and the emotions at quitting forever the scene of so many triumphs, and of long standing associations—for the Haymarket Company was termed " the happy family "—season after season for many years rarely witnessing any change amongst the members—that she sudden y became speechless, and three days afterwards, July 15th, 1850, she expired.

Of Mr. O. Smith's popularity and fame, for his deep voice and demoniacal laugh, I may mention a little incident. Some years since, I produced in London an extravaganza called "The Three Princes," and I am happy to say it met with the greatest possible success. I introduced in it an allusion to his voice. The evil genius of the piece threatens utter annihilation to one of the princes, to which the reply came:

> " Destroy me, kin and kith !
> You speak exactly like the Adelphi Smith !"

and so well and so widely known was the actor and his voice, that during a run of nearly two hundred nights, the allusion and imitation never once failed to bring forth a hearty laugh.

With reference to the character of Sir John Vesey, it is interesting to observe that "truth is stranger than fiction." He says, in the first scene, "If you have no merit or money of your own, you must trade on the merits and money of other people." In a recent great law case in England, "The Tichborne Case," the trial of which lasted nearly twelve months, an old pocket book was produced in evidence, in which the claimant to the title and estates (afterwards sentenced to fourteen years imprisonment for perjury and forgery) had written "some people has plenty of money and no brains, and some people has plenty of brains and no money," therefore, he held it was the duty of the latter to prey upon the former. He was evidently a vulgar disciple of the Sir John Vesey school, of which there are specimens to be met with everywhere.

Mr. Macready was followed in the character of Alfred Evelyn, by all those who had followed him in the Lady of Lyons; Charles Kean, Phelps, Anderson, Creswick, and a host of others previously mentioned, who were as successful in this as in the previous plays.

As before stated, Money was first produced in America at the Old Park Theatre, New York, Feb. 1st, 1841, with an excellent cast.

Mr. Hield, who played the hero, was a gentlemanly and intellectual actor; he made a great hit, and for many years afterwards repeated the character with continued success.

Mr. Chippendale as Sir John Vesey, and Mrs. Chippendale as Georgina, were also most successful, whilst Mrs. Maeder as Clara Douglas, and Mrs. Vernon as the warm hearted Lady Franklin, added greatly to the triumph of the play.

It was afterwards produced at the Chatham Theatre, situated on Chatham street between Roosevelt and James streets, and at the Broadway, which was situated on Broadway between Pearl street and Anthony (now Worth) street, with the following cast:

	Chatham Theatre, Sept. 4, 1843.	Broadway Theatre, Nov. 4, 1847.
Alfred Evelyn	Mr. HIELD.	Mr. G. VANDENHOFF.
Sir John Vesey	Mr. GREENE.	Mr. H. WALLACK.
Lord Glossmore	Mr. BOOTH, JR.	Mr. FREDERICKS.
Sir Frederick Blount	Mr. FIELD.	Mr. LESTER.
Stout	Mr. COLLINS.	Mr. E. SHAW.
Graves	Mr. BURTON.	Mr. VACHE.
Captain Dudley Smooth	Mr. STEVENS.	Mr. DAWSON.
Clara Douglas	Mrs. G. JONES.	Miss F. WALLACK.
Lady Franklin	Mrs. RIVERS.	Mrs. WINSTANLEY.
Georgina	Miss KIRBY.	Mrs. SERGEANT.

And also on September 16, 1857, at Burton's New Theatre, when Mr. Murdoch played Alfred Evelyn, Mr. Burton, Graves, and Mrs. W. H. Smith, Lady Franklin.

But perhaps as fine and almost as good a representation of the comedy was that produced at Wallack's Theatre, New York, Jan. 17, 1874, with the following excellent cast:

Alfred Evelyn..Mr. LESTER WALLACK.
Sir John Vesey..Mr. J. W. CARROLL.
Lord Glossmore, ...Mr. J. W. FERGUSON.
Sir Frederick Blount......................................Mr. W. R. FLOYD.
Benjamin Stout..Mr. JOHN BROUGHAM.
Graves..Mr. HARRY BECKETT.
Captain Dudley Smooth.....................................Mr. J. B. POLK.
Mr. Sharp...Mr. G. F. BROWNE.
Old Member...Mr. T. C. MILLS.
Clara Douglas..Miss JEFFREYS LEWIS.
Lady Franklin...Madame PONISI.
Georgina..Miss DORA GOLDTHWAITE.

Having been present upon innumerable occasions of the representations of this play, and witnessed the performance of nearly all the Alfred Evelyns on the London boards, I have no hesitation in saying I never, as a whole, saw the play better mounted or acted. The Alfred Evelyn of Mr. Lester Wallack will bear comparison with any; if we could only have the pleasure of making him a few years younger it would enhance the beauty of the performance; but one could afford to put aside that little drawback; it was fully compensated for by the fine delivery of the text, and the intellect and bearing of one of nature's nobleman, such as Alfred Evelyn is supposed to be, and the actor is.

Mr. John Brougham's *Stout*, Mr. Harry Beckett's *Graves*, Mr. W. R. Floyd's *Sir Frederick Blount*, were all most admirably rendered. Miss Jeffreys Lewis made an excellent *Clara Douglas*, and as *Lady Franklin*, Madame Ponisi well sustained her reputation, whilst Miss Dora Goldthwaite as *Georgina* was all that was needed. Indeed all engaged were good. As I have said in my former remarks, so I say of this play—not one jot of brilliancy and effect has been lost in transferring it to the American boards.   J. M. K.

MONEY.

ACT I.

SCENE I.—*A drawing-room in* Sir John Vesey's *house ; folding doors* c., *which open on another drawing-room. To the right a table, with the Morning Post newspaper, books, etc. ; to the left, a sofa and writing table. The furniture tasteful and costly.*

Sir John *and* Georgina *discovered,* R. C.

Sir John (*reading a letter edged with black*). Yes, he says at two precisely. "Dear Sir John, as since the death of my sainted Maria,"— Hum !—that's his wife ; she made him a martyr, and now he makes her a saint !

Geor. Well, as since her death ?—

Sir J. (*reading*). "I have been living in chambers, where I cannot so well invite ladies, you will allow me to bring Mr. Sharp, the lawyer, to read the will of the late Mr. Mordaunt (to which I am appointed executor) at your house—your daughter being the nearest relation. I shall be with you at two precisely.—Henry Graves."

Geor. And you really think I shall be uncle Mordaunt's heiress ? And that the fortune he made in India is half a million ?

Sir J. Ay! I have no doubt you will be the richest heiress in England. But sit down, my dear Georgy—my dear girl. (Georgina *sits* R. H. *of table,* Sir John L. H.) Upon this happy—I mean melancholy—occasion, I feel that I may trust you with a secret. You see this fine house —our fine servants—our fine plate—our fine dinners ; every one thinks Sir John Vesey a rich man.

Geor. And are you not, papa ?

Sir J. Not a bit of it—all humbug, child—all humbug, upon my soul ! There are two rules in life—First, men are not valued for what they *are*, but what they *seem* to be. Secondly, if you have no merit or money of your own, you must trade on the merits and money of other people. My father got the title by services in the army, and died penniless. On the strength of his services I got a pension of £400 a year ; on the strength of £400 a year I took credit for £800 ; on the strength of £800 a year I married your mother with £10,000 ; on the strength of £10,000 I took credit for £40,000, and paid Dicky Gossip three guineas a week to go about everywhere calling me "Stingy Jack !"

Geor. Ha! ha! A disagreeable nickname.

Sir J. But a valuable reputation. When a man is called stingy, it is as much as calling him rich ; and when a man's called rich, why he's a man universally respected. On the strength of my respectability I wheedled a constituency, changed my politics, resigned my seat to a minister, who, to a man of such stake in the country, could offer nothing less in return than a patent office of £2,000 a year. That's the way to succeed in life. Humbug, my dear—all humbug, upon my soul!

GEOR. I must say that you—

SIR J. Know the world, to be sure. Now, for your fortune—as I spend more than my income, I can have nothing to leave you; yet, even without counting your uncle, you have always passed for an heiress on the credit of your expectations from the savings of "Stingy Jack." Apropos of a husband; you know we thought of Sir Frederick Blount.

GEOR. Ah, papa, he is charming.

SIR J. Hem! He *was so*, my dear, before we knew your poor uncle was dead; but an heiress such as you will be should look out for a duke. Where the deuce is Evelyn this morning? (*rises, puts back the chair, goes to* L. *table, marks the letter and puts it in his pocket.*)

GEOR. I've not seen him, papa. What a strange character he is—so sarcastic; and yet he can be agreeable. (*puts back her chair and then goes* R.)

SIR J. A humorist—a cynic! One never knows how to take him. My private secretary—a poor cousin, has not got a shilling, and yet, hang me, if he does not keep us all at a sort of a distance.

GEOR. But why do you take him to live with us, papa, since there's no good to be got by it?

SIR J. There you are wrong; he has a great deal of talent; prepares my speeches, writes my pamphlets, looks up my calculations. Besides, he *is* our cousin—he has no salary; kindness to a poor relation always tells well in the world; and benevolence is a useful virtue—particularly when you can have it for nothing. With our other cousin, Clara, it was different; her father thought fit to leave me her guardian, though she had not a penny—a mere useless encumbrance; so, you see, I got my half-sister, Lady Franklin, to take her off my hands.

GEOR. How much longer is Lady Franklin's visit to be? (*at table* R., *takes up paper, reads until she speaks to* EVELYN.)

SIR J. I don't know, my dear; the longer the better—for her husband left her a good deal of money at her own disposal. Ah, here she comes!

Enter LADY FRANKLIN *and* CLARA, C. R.

My dear sister, we were just loud in your praises. But how's this—not in mourning?

LADY F. Why should I go in mourning for a man I never saw?

SIR J. Still there may be a legacy.

LADY F. Then there'll be less cause for affliction! Ha, ha! my dear Sir John, I'm one of those who think feelings a kind of property, and never take credit for them upon false pretences. (*crosses to table* L., *sits.*)

SIR J. (*aside,* L.). Very silly woman! (*aloud*) But, Clara, I see you are more attentive to the proper decorum; yet you are very, *very*, VERY distantly connected with the deceased—a third cousin, I think?

CLARA. Mr. Mordaunt once assisted my father, and these poor robes are all the gratitude I can show him. (*goes to* L. *table and sits.*)

SIR J. (*aside*). Gratitude! humph! I am afraid the minx has got expectations.

LADY F. So, Mr. Graves is the executor—the will is addressed to him? The same Mr. Graves who is always in black, always lamenting his ill-fortune and his sainted Maria, who led him the life of a dog?

SIR J. The very same. His liveries are black—his carriage is black —he always rides a black galloway—and faith, if he ever marry again, I think he will show his respect to the sainted Maria by marrying a black woman.

Lady F. Ha! ha! we shall see. (*aside*) Poor Graves, I always liked him; he made an excellent husband. (*down* c.)

Enter Evelrn, c. l., *seats himself* l. *of* r. *table, and takes up a book unobserved.*

Sir J. What a crowd of relations this will brings to light! Mr. Stout, the Political Economist—Lord Glossmore——

Lady F. Whose grandfather kept a pawnbroker's shop, and who, accordingly, entertains the profoundest contempt for everything popular, *parvenu*, and plebeian.

Sir J. Sir Frederick Blount——

Lady F. Sir Fwedewick Blount, who objects to the letter *r* as being too *wough*, and therefore d*w*ops its acquaintance; one of the new class of prudent young gentlemen, who, not having spirits and constitution for the hearty excesses of their predecessors, intrench themselves in the dignity of a lady-like languor. A man of fashion in the last century was riotous and thoughtless—in this he is tranquil and egotistical. He never does anything that is silly, or says anything that is wise. I beg your pardon, my dear; I believe Sir Frederick is an admirer of yours, provided, on reflection, he does not see "what harm it could do him" to fall in love with your beauty and expectations. Then, too, our poor cousin the scholar—(Clara *touches* Lady Franklin, *and points to* Evelyn. *All turn and look at him*) Oh, Mr. Evelyn, there you are! (*resumes her seat.*)

Sir J. (*going up to* Evelyn, r. c.). Evelyn—the very person I wanted; where have you been all day? Have you seen to those papers?—have you written my epitaph on poor Mordaunt?—Latin, you know?—have you reported my speech at Exeter Hall?—have you looked out the debates on the Customs?—and—oh, have you mended up all the old pens in the study?

Geor. (r. *of* r. *table*). And have you brought me the black floss silk? —have you been to Storr's for my ring?—and, as we cannot go out on this melancholy occasion, did you call at Hookham's for the last H. B. and the Comic Annual?

Lady F. (*rises and goes to* Evelyn). And did you see what was really the matter with my bay horse?—did you get me the opera-box?—did you buy my little Charley his peg-top?

Evelyn (*always reading*). Certainly, Paley is right upon that point; for, put the syllogism thus—(*looking up*) Ma'am—sir—Miss Vesey—you want something of me?—Paley observes, that to assist even the undeserving tends to the better regulation of our charitable feelings.—No apologies—I am quite at your service. (*shuts the book and comes forward.*)

Sir J. Now he's in one of his humors!

Lady F. (*down* r.). You allow him strange liberties, Sir John.

Eve. (c.). You will be the less surprised at that, madam, when I inform you that Sir John allows me nothing else. I am now about to draw on his benevolence.

Lady F. I beg your pardon, sir, and like your spirit. Sir John, I'm in the way, I see; for I know your benevolence is so delicate that you never allow any one to detect it!　　　　　　[*Retires and goes off.* c. l.

Eve. I could not do your commissions to-day—I have been to visit a poor woman, who was my nurse and my mother's last friend. She is very poor—*very*—sick—dying—and she owes six months' rent!

Sir J. (l.). You know I should be most happy to do anything for yourself. But the nurse—(*aside*) Some people's nurses are always ill! (*aloud*) There are so many impostors about! We'll talk of it to-morrow.

(EVELYN *goes to the table*, L.) This mournful occasion takes up all of my attention. (*looking at his watch*) Bless me ! so late ! I've letters to write, and—none of the pens are mended !   [*Exit*, R.

GEOR. (*taking out her purse*, R.). I think I will give it to him—and yet if I don't get the fortune. after all !—Papa allows me so little !—then I *must* have those earrings. (*puts up the purse*) Mr. Evelyn, what is the address of your nurse ?

EVE. (*writes at* L. *table, and gives it—aside*). She has a good heart with all her foibles ! (*aloud*) Ah ! Miss Vesey, if that poor woman had not closed the eyes of my lost mother, Alfred Evelyn would not have been this beggar to your father.

GEOR. (*reading*). "Mrs. Staunton, 14 Amos street, Pentonville."

(CLARA, *at the table, writes down the address as she hears* GEORGINA *read it.*)

GEOR. I will certainly attend to it—(*aside*) it I get the fortune. (EVE-LYN *goes up* R.)

SIR J. (*calling, without*). Georgy, I say !

GEOR. Yes, papa !   '   [*Exit*, R.

EVELYN *has seated himself again at the table—to the right,—and leans his face on his hands.*

CLARA. His noble spirit bowed to this ! Ah, at least here I may give him comfort. (*sits down to write*) But he will recognize my hand.

Re-enter LADY FRANKLIN, C.

LADY F. (*looking over her shoulder*). What bill are you paying, Clara ? —putting up a bank-note ?

CLARA. Hush!—O, Lady Franklin, you are the kindest of human beings. This is for a poor person—I would not have her know whence it came, or she would refuse it ! Would you ?—No—No—he knows *her* handwriting also !

LADY F. Will I—what ?—give the money myself ?—with pleasure ! Poor Clara—why, this covers all your savings—and I am so rich !

CLARA. Nay, I would wish to do all myself ! It is a pride—a duty— it is a joy ; and I have so few joys ! But hush!—this way. (*they retire into the inner room and converse in dumb show.*)

EVE. (*seated*). And thus must I grind out my life for ever ! I am ambitious, and Poverty drags me down ; I have learning, and Poverty makes me the drudge of fools ! I love, and Poverty stands like a spectre before the altar ! But no, no—if, as I believe, I am but loved again, I will—will—what ?—turn opium eater, and dream of the Eden I may never enter ? (LADY FRANKLIN *and* CLARA *advance*, C.)

CLARA. But you must be sure that Evelyn never knows that I sent this money to his nurse.

LADY F. (*to* CLARA). Never fear—I will get my maid to copy and direct this—she writes well, and *her* hand will never be discovered. I will have it done and sent instantly.   [*Exit*, R.

CLARA *advances to the front of stage, and seats herself*, R. C ; EVELYN *reading. Enter* SIR FREDERICK BLOUNT, C. L. ; *he comes down*, L. C.

BLOUNT. No one in the woom !—Oh, Miss Douglas ! Pway don't let me disturb you. Where is Miss Vesey—Georgina ? (*taking* CLARA'S *chair as she rises.*)

EVE. (*looking up, gives* CLARA *a chair, and reseats himself.* · *Aside*) Insolent puppy !

CLARA. Shall I tell her you are here, Sir Frederick?

BLOUNT. Not for the world. Vewy pwetty girl this companion! (*sits* L. C.)

CLARA. What did you think of the Panorama the other day, Cousin Evelyn?

EVE. (*reading*).
> " I cannot talk with civet in the room,
>   A fine puss gentleman that's all perfume !"

Rather good lines these.

BLOUNT. Sir !

EVE. (*offering the book*). Don't you think so ?—Cowper.

BLOUNT. (*declining the book*). Cowper !

EVE. Cowper.

BLOUNT (*shrugging his shoulders, to* CLARA). Stwange person, Mr. Evelyn!—quite a chawacter!—Indeed the Panowama gives you no idea of Naples—a delightful place. I make it a wule to go there evewy second year—I'm vewy fond of twavelling. You'd like Wome (Rome)—bad inns, but vewy fine wuins; gives you quite a taste for that sort of thing !

EVE. (*reading*).
> " How much a dunce that has been sent to roam
>   Excels a dunce that has been kept at home !"

BLOUNT. Sir ?

EVE. Cowper.

BLOUNT (*aside*). That fellow Cowper says vewy odd things! Humph! it is beneath me to quawwell. (*aloud*) It will not take long to wead the will, I suppose. Poor old Mordaunt!—I am his nearest male welation. He was vewy eccentwic. (*draws his chair nearer*) By the way, Miss Douglas, did you wemark my cuwicle ? It is bwinging cuwicles into fashion. I should be most happy if you will allow me to dwive you out. Nay—nay—I should, upon my word. (*trying to take her hand.*)

EVE (*starting up*). A wasp!—a wasp!—just going to settle. Take care of the wasp, Miss Douglas!

BLOUNT. A wasp—where!—don't bwing it this way—some people don't mind them ! I've a particlar dislike to wasps ; they sting damnably !

EVE. I beg pardon—it's only a gadfly.

Enter PAGE, R.

PAGE. Sir John will be happy to see you in his study, Sir Frederick.
[*Exit* PAGE, C. L.

BLOUNT. Vewy well. (*rises and goes* R) Upon my word, there is something vewy nice about this girl. To be sure. I love Georgina—but if this one would take a fancy to me—(*thoughtfully*)—Well, I don't see what harm it could do me! *Au plaisir ?*   [*Exit*, R.

CLARA *takes her chair to* R. *of* L. *table.*

EVE. Clara !

CLARA. Cousin ! (*coming forward*, L.)

EVE. And you, too, are a dependant ?

CLARA. But on Lady Franklin, who seeks to make me forget it.

EVE. Ay, but can the world forget it ? This insolent condescension—this coxcombry of admiration—more galling than the arrogance of contempt! Look you now—Robe Beauty in silk and cashmere—hand Virtue into her chariot—lackey their caprices—wrap them from the winds—fence them round with a golden circle—and Virtue and Beauty are as

goddesses both to peasant and to prince. Strip them of the adjuncts—
see Beauty and Virtue poor—dependant—solitary—walking the world
defenceless! oh, *then* the devotion changes its character—the same
crowd gather eagerly around—fools—fops—libertines—not to worship
at the shrine, but to sacrifice the victim!

CLARA. My cousin, you are cruel!—I can smile at the pointless inso-
lence.

EVE. Smile—and he took your hand! Oh, Clara, you know not the
tortures that I suffer hourly! When others approach you—young—fair
—rich—the sleek darlings of the world—I accuse you of your very
beauty—I writhe beneath every smile that you bestow. (CLARA, *about to
speak*) No—speak not—my heart has broken its silence, and you shall
hear the rest. For you I have endured the weary bondage of this house
—the fool's gibe—the hireling's sneer—the bread purchased by toils
that should have led me to loftier ends; yes, to see you—hear you—
breathe the same air—be ever at hand—that if others slighted, from one
at least you might receive the luxury of respect—for this—for this I
have lingered, suffered, and forborne. Oh, Clara! we are orphans both
—friendless both; you are all in the world to me; (*she turns away*) turn
not away—my very soul speaks in these words—I LOVE YOU! (*kneels.*)

CLARA. No—Evelyn—Alfred—no! Say it not; think it not! it were
madness.

EVE. Madness!—nay, hear me yet. I am poor, dependant—a beggar for bread to a dying servant. True! But I have a heart of iron. I
have knowledge—patience—health—and my love for you gives me at
last ambition! I have trifled with my own energies till now, for I despised all things till I loved you. With you to toil for—your step to
support—your path to smooth—and I—I, poor Alfred Evelyn—promise
at last to win for you even fame and fortune! Do not withdraw your
hand—*this* hand—shall it not be mine?

CLARA. Ah, Evelyn! Never—never! (*crosses to* R.)

EVE. Never? (*rises.*)

CLARA. Forget this folly; our union is impossible, and to talk of love
were to deceive both!

EVE. (*bitterly*). Because I am poor!

CLARA. And *I too!* A marriage of privation—of penury—of days that
dread the morrow! I have seen such a lot! Never return to this again.

EVE. Enough—you are obeyed. I deceived myself—ha—ha! I fancied that I too was loved. I, whose youth is already half gone with care
and toil—whose mind is soured—whom nobody *can* love—who ought to
have loved no one!

CLARA (*aside*). And if it were only ⊥ to suffer, or perhaps to starve!
Oh, what shall I say? (*aloud*) Evelyn—cousin!

EVE. Madam.

CLARA. Alfred—I—I——

EVE. Reject me?

CLARA. Yes. It is past!   [*Exit*, R.

EVE. Let me think. It was yesterday her hand trembled when mine
touched it. And the rose I gave her—yes, she pressed her lips to it
once when she seemed as if she saw me not. But it was a trap—a trick
—for I was as poor then as now. This will be a jest for them all!
Well, courage! it is but a poor heart that a coquette's contempt can
break. (*retires up to the table*, R.)

Enter LORD GLOSSMORE, *preceded by* PAGE, C. L.

PAGE. I will tell Sir John, my Lord. (*Exit*, R. EVELYN *takes up the
newspaper.*)

GLOSS. The secretary—hum! Fine day, sir; any news from the east?

EVE. Yes—all the wise men have gone back there!

SERVANT, C. L., *announces* MR. STOUT, R.

GLOSS. Ha! ha!—not all, for here comes Mr. Stout, the great political economist.

Enter STOUT, C. L.

STOUT (R. C). Good morning, Glossmore.

GLOSS. (L.). *Glossmore!*—the parvenu!

STOUT. Afraid I might be late—been detained at the vestry—astonishing how ignorant the English poor are! Took me an hour and a half to beat it into the head of a stupid old widow, with nine children, that to allow her three shillings a week was against all rules of public morality. (EVELYN *rises and comes down*, R.)

EVE. Excellent—admirable—your hand, sir!

GLOSS. What! you approve such doctrines, Mr. Evelyn? Are old women only fit to be starved?

EVE. Starved! popular delusion! Observe, my lord, (*crosses*, C.) to squander money upon those who starve is only to afford encouragement to starvation!

STOUT. A very superior person that!

GLOSS. Atrocious principles! Give me the good old times, when it was the duty of the rich to succor the distressed.

EVE. On second thoughts, *you* are right, my lord. I, too, know a poor woman—ill—dying—in want. Shall *she*, too, perish?

GLOSS. Perish! horrible—in a Christian country! Perish! Heaven forbid!

EVE. (*holding out his hand*). What, then, will you give her?

GLOSS. Ahem! Sir, the parish ought to give.

STOUT. By no means!

GLOSS. By all means!

STOUT. No!—no!—no! Certainly not! (*with great vehemence.*)

GLOSS. No! no! But I say, yes! yes! And if the parish refuse to maintain the poor, the only way left to a man of firmness and resolution, holding the principles that I do, and adhering to the constitution of our fathers, is to force the poor *on* the parish by never giving them a farthing one's self.

STOUT. No!—no!—no!

GLOSS. Yes!—yes!—yes!

EVE. Gentlemen!—gentlemen!—perhaps Sir John will decide. (*pointing to* SIR JOHN *as he enters, and retires to table, takes up a book, reads.*)

Enter SIR JOHN, LADY FRANKLIN, GEORGINA, BLOUNT, PAGE, R. PAGE *goes off*, C. L. LADY FRANKLIN *goes to table*, L., *and sits.*

SIR J. How d'ye do? Ah! how d'ye do, gentlemen? This is a most melancholy meeting! The poor deceased! what a man he was!

BLOUNT (R.). I was chwistened Fwederick after him! He was my first cousin.

SIR J. (C.). And Georgina his own niece—next of kin! an excellent man, though odd—a kind heart, but no liver! I sent him twice a year thirty dozen of the Cheltenham waters. It's a comfort to reflect on these little attentions at such a time.

STOUT. And I, too, sent him the parliamentary debates regularly,

bound in calf. He was my second cousin—sensible man—and a fol-
lower of Malthus; never married to increase the surplus population, and
fritter away his money on his own children. And now——

EVE. He reaps the benefit of celibacy in the prospective gratitude of
every cousin he had in the world!

LADY F. Ha! ha! ha!

SIR J. Hush! hush! decency, Lady Franklin; decency!

Enter PAGE, C. L.

PAGE. Mr. Graves—Mr. Sharp.

SIR J. Oh, here's Mr. Graves; that's Sharp the lawyer, who brought
the will from Calcutta.

Enter MR. GRAVES. *and* MR. SHARP, *who goes immediately to* L. *table, and*
prepares his papers.

Chorus of SIR JOHN, GLOSSMORE, BLOUNT, STOUT. Ah, sir—ah, Mr.
Graves! (GEORGINA *holds her handkerchief to her eyes.*)

SIR J. A sad occasion!

GRAVES. But everything in life is sad. Be comforted, Miss Vesey!
True, you have lost an uncle; but I—I have lost a wife—such a wife!—
the first of her sex—and the second cousin of the defunct!

Enter SERVANTS, C.

Excuse me, Sir John; at the sight of your mourning my wounds bleed
afresh. (SERVANTS *hand round wine and cake.*)

SIR J. Take some refreshment—a glass of wine.

GRAVES. Thank you!—(Very fine sherry!) Ah! my poor sainted
Maria! Sherry was *her* wine! everything reminds me of Maria! Ah,
Lady Franklin! *you* knew her. Nothing in life can charm me now.
(*aside*) A monstrous fine woman that!

SIR J. And now to business. (*they each take a chair*) Evelyn, you may
retire. (*All sit.* SERVANTS *retire,* C. EVELYN *rises.*)

SHARP (*looking at his notes*). Evelyn—any relation to Alfred Evelyn?
(*to* EVELYN, *who is going,* C.)

EVE. The same.

SHARP. Cousin to the deceased, seven times removed. Be seated, sir;
there may be some legacy, though trifling; all the relations, however
distant, should be present. (EVELYN *reluctantly resumes his seat.*)

LADY F. Then Clara is related—I will go for her.   [*Exit,* R.

GEOR. Ah, Mr. Evelyn! I hope you will come in for something—a
few hundreds, or even more.

SIR J. Silence! Hush! Wugh! Ugh! Attention!

While the Lawyer opens the will, re-enter LADY FRANKLIN *and* CLARA. *They*
cross behind the characters to L., *up the stage, and sit.*

Disposition of Characters.

EVELYN.   LADY FRANKLIN, CLARA.
            SIR JOHN.   STOUT.   GLOSSMORE.
BLOUNT.   GEORGINA.   GRAVES.   SHARP.
    R.   L.

SHARP. The will is very short—being all personal property. He was a man that always came to the point.

SIR J. I wish there were more like him! (*groans and shakes his head.*)

SHARP (*reading*). " I, Frederick James Mordaunt, of Calcutta, being, at the present date, of sound mind, though infirm body, do hereby give, will, and bequeath—Imprimis, To my second cousin, Benjamin Stout, Esq., of Pall Mall, London—(STOUT *puts a large silk handkerchief to his eyes. Chorus exhibit lively emotion*) Being the value of the Parliamentary Debates with which he has been pleased to trouble me for some time past—deducting the carriage thereof, which he always forgot to pay— the sum of £14 2s. 4d." (STOUT *removes the handkerchief ; Chorus breathe more freely.*)

STOUT. Eh, what ?—£14 ? Oh, hang the old miser !

SIR J. Decency—decency ! Proceed, sir. Go on, sir, go on.

SHARP. " Item.—To Sir Frederick Blount, Baronet, my nearest male relative—" (*Chorus exhibit lively emotion.*)

BLOUNT. Poor old boy ! (GEORGINA *puts her arm over* BLOUNT'S *chair.*)

SHARP. " Being, as I am informed, the best-dressed young gentleman in London, and in testimony to the only merit I ever heard he possessed, the sum of £500 to buy a dressing-case." (*Chorus breathe more freely ;* GEORGINA *catches her father's eye, and removes her arm.*)

BLOUNT (*laughing confusedly*). Ha ! ha ! ha ! Vewy poor wit—low !— vewy—vewy low !

SIR J. Silence, now, will you ? Go on, sir, go on.

SHARP. " Item.—To Charles Lord Glossmore—who asserts that he is my relation—my collection of dried butterflies, and the pedigree of the Mordaunts from the reign of King John. (*Chorus as before.*)

GLOSS. Butterflies!—Pedigree!—I disown the Plebeian !

SIR J. (*angrily*). Upon my word, this is too revolting ! Decency ! Go on, sir, go on.

SHARP. " Item.—To Sir John Vesey, Baronet, Knight of the Guelph, F.R.S., F.S.A., etc." (*Chorus as before.*)

SIR J. Hush ! *Now* it is really interesting !

SHARP. " Who married my sister, and who sends me every year the Cheltenham waters, which nearly gave me my death, I bequeath—the empty bottles."

SIR J. Why, the ungrateful, rascally old——

LADY F. Decency, Sir John—decency !

CHORUS. Decency, Sir John—decency !

SHARP. " Item.—To Henry Graves, Esq., of the Albany—" (*Chorus as before.*)

GRAVES. Pooh ! gentlemen—my usual luck—not even a ring, I dare swear.

SHARP. " The sum of £5,000 in the Three per Cents."

LADY F. I wish you joy !

GRAVES. Joy—pooh ! Three per Cents. ! Funds sure to go ! Had it been *land*, now—though only an acre !—just like my luck.

SHARP. " Item.—To my niece, Georgina Vesey——(*chorus as before.*)

SIR J. Ah, now it comes !

SHARP. " The sum of £10,000 India Stock, being, with her father's reputed savings, as much as a single woman ought to possess."

SIR J. And what the devil, then, does the old fool do with all his money ?

CHORUS. Really, Sir John, this is too revolting. Decency ! Hush !

SHARP. " And, with the aforesaid legacies and exceptions, I do will and bequeath the whole of my fortune, in India Stock, Bonds, Exchequer Bills, Three per Cent. Consols, and in the Bank of Calcutta (constituting him hereby sole residuary legatee and joint executor with the aforesaid Henry Graves, Esq.), to—Alfred Evelyn, now, or formerly, of Trinity College, Cambridge—(*all turn to* EVELYN; *universal excitement.* EVELYN *starts up, closes his book, and casts it upon the table*) Being, I am told, an oddity, like myself—the only one of my relations who never fawned on me ; and who, having known privation, may the better employ wealth." (*all rise.* EVELYN *advances,* C., *as if in a dream*) And now, sir, I have only to wish you joy, and give you this letter from the deceased —I believe it is important. (*gives letter to* EVELYN.)

EVE. (*aside*). Ah, Clara, if you had but loved me !

CLARA (*turning away*). And his wealth, even more than poverty, separates us for ever ! (OMNES *crowd round to congratulate* EVELYN.)

SIR J. (*aside to* GEORGINA). Go, child, put a good face on it—he's an immense match ! (*aloud*) My dear fellow, I wish you joy; you are a great man now—a very great man! · I wish you joy. (*shakes his hand very warmly.*)

EVE. (*aside*). And *her* voice alone is silent !

GLOSS If I can be of any use to you——

STOUT. Or I, sir——

BLOUNT. Or I ! Shall I put you up at the clubs ?

SHARP. You will want a man of business. I transacted all Mr. Mordaunt's affairs.

SIR J. Tush, tush ! Mr. Evelyn is at home *here*—always looked upon him as a son ! Nothing in the world we would not do for him ! Nothing !

EVE. Nothing ! then lend me £10 for my old nurse. (*Chorus put their hands in their pockets.*)

CURTAIN.

ACT II.

SCENE I.—*An anteroom in* EVELYN'S *new house ;* MR. SHARP *writing at a desk,* L., *books and parchments before him*—MR. CRIMSON, *the portrait painter ;* MR. GRABB, *the publisher ;* MR. MACSTUCCO, *the architect ;* MR. TABOURET, *the upholsterer ;* MR. MACFINCH, *the silversmith ;* MR. PATENT, *the coachmaker ;* MR. KITE, *the horse-dealer ; and* MR. FRANTZ, *the tailor.*

PATENT (*to* FRANTZ, *showing him a drawing*). Yes, sir ; this is the Evelyn vis-à-vis ! No one more the fashion than Mr. Evelyn. Money makes the man, sir.

FRANTZ. But de tailor, de schneider make de gentleman ! It is Mr. Frantz, of St. James',who take his measure and his cloth, and who make de fine handsome noblemen and gentry, where de faders and de mutters make only de ugly little naked boys !

MACSTUC (L. C.). He's a mon o' teeste, Mr. Evelyn. He taulks o' buying a veela (villa), just to pool down and build oop again. Ah, Mr. MacFinch ! a design for a piece of pleete, eh ?

MACFINCH (L., *showing the drawing*). Yees, sir ; the shield o' Alexander the Great to hold ices and lemonade ! It will coost two thousand poon' !

MACSTUC. And it's dirt cheap—ye're Scotch, arn't ye ?

MACFINCH. Aberdounshire !—scraitch me, and I'll scraitch you !

Enter EVELYN, C. D. L.

EVE. A levee, as usual. Good day. Ah, Tabouret, (TABOURET *presents a drawing*) your designs for the draperies; very well. (*Exit* TABOURET, R.) And what do you want, Mr. Crimson?

CRIM. (R). Sir, if you'd let me take your portrait, it would make my fortune. Every one says you're the finest judge of paintings.

EVE. Of paintings! paintings! Are you sure I'm a judge of paintings?

CRIM. Oh, sir, didn't you buy the great Corregio for £4,000?

EVE. True—I see. So £4,000 makes me an excellent judge of paintings. I'll call on you, Mr. Crimson—good day. (*Exit* CRIMSON, R. EVELYN *turns to the rest who surround him.*)

KITE. Thirty young horses from Yorkshire, sir!

PATENT (*showing drawing*). The Evelyn vis-à-vis!

MACFINCH (*showing drawing*). The Evelyn salver!

FRANTZ (*opening his bundle, and with dignity*). Sare, I have brought de coat—de great Evelyn coat.

EVE. Oh, go to—that is, go home. Make me as celebrated for a vis-à-vis, salvers, furniture, and coats, as I already am for painting, and shortly shall be for poetry. I resign myself to you—go! (*crosses.* L.)

[*Exeunt* MACFINCH, PATENT, *etc.*, R.*

Enter STOUT, R., *he places his hat on* R. *table.*

EVE. Stout, you look heated!

STOUT. I hear that you have just bought the great Groginhole property.

EVE. It is true. Sharp says it's a bargain.

STOUT. Well, my dear friend Hopkins, member for Groginhole, can't live another month—but the interests of mankind forbid regret for individuals! The patriot Popkins intends to start for the borough the instant Hopkins is dead—your interests will secure his election. Now is your time! put yourself forward in the march of enlightenment. (*turns and sees* GLOSSMORE) By all that is bigoted, here comes Glossmore! (*goes up the stage and listens.*)

Enter GLOSSMORE, R. EVELYN *crosses to meet him.*

GLOSS. So lucky to find you at home! Hopkins, of Groginhole, is not long for this world. Popkins, the brewer, is already canvassing underhand (so very ungentlemanlike!). Keep your interest for young Lord Cipher—a most valuable candidate. This is an awful moment—the CONSTITUTION depends on his return! Vote for Cipher.

STOUT (L.). Popkins is your man!

EVE. (*musingly*). Cipher and Popkins—Popkins and Cipher! Enlightenment and Popkins—Cipher and the Constitution! I AM puzzled! Stout, I am not known at Groginhole.

STOUT. Your *property's* known there!

EVE. But purity of election—independence of votes——

---

* The dialogue of this scene, up to this point, is sometimes omitted, and when that is the case, begin thus:—

Enter STOUT, *preceded by a* SERVANT, R.

SERV. I'll tell my master you wish to see him. Oh! Mr. Evelyn is here, sir!

Enter EVELYN, L.

STOUT. To be sure ; Cipher bribes *abominably.* Frustrate his schemes —preserve the liberties of the borough—turn every man out of his house who votes against enlightenment and Popkins !

EVE. Right !—down with those who take the liberty to admire any liberty except *our* liberty ! That *is* liberty !

GLOSS. Cipher has a stake in the country—will have £50,000 a year —Cipher will never give a vote without considering beforehand how people of £50,000 a year will be affected by the motion.

EVE. Right! for as without law there would be no property, so to be the law for property is the only proper property of law! That *is* law !

STOUT. Popkins is all for economy—there's a sad waste of the public money—they give the Speaker £5,000 a year, when I've a brother-in-law, who takes the chair at the vestry, and who assures me confidentially he'd consent to be Speaker for half the money !

GLOSS. Enough, Mr. Stout. Mr. Evelyn has too mucn at stake for a leveller.

STOUT. And too much sense for a bigot.

GLOSS. Bigot, sir ?

STOUT. Yes, sir, bigot!

EVE. Mr. Evelyn has no politics at all ! Did you ever play at *battledore ?*

BOTH. Battledore !

EVE. Battledore !—that is a contest between two parties ; both parties knock about something with singular skill—something is kept up— high—low—here—there—everywhere—nowhere ! How grave are the players ! how anxious the bystanders ! how noisy the battledores ! But when this something falls to the ground, only fancy—it's nothing but cork and feather ! Go, and play by yourselves—I'm no hand at it ! (*crosses,* L)

STOUT (*aside*). Sad ignorance !—Aristocrat ! (*crosses to* R. C.)

GLOSS. (*aside*). Heartless principles !—Parvenu ! (*goes up the stage.*)

STOUT. Then you don't go *against* us ? I'll bring Popkins to-morrow. (*goes to* R. *table, gets his hat.*)

GLOSS. Keep yourself free till I present Cipher to you !

STOUT. I must go to inquire after Hopkins. The return of Popkins will be an era in history !   [*Exit,* R.

GLOSS. I must be off to the club—the eyes of the country are upon Groginhole. If Cipher fail, the constitution is gone !   [*Exit,* R

EVE. (R. C.). Both sides alike ! Money *versus* Man !—poor man !— Sharp, come here—(SHARP *advances*) let me look at you ! You are my agent, my lawyer, my man of business. I believe you honest ;—but what *is* honesty ? where does it exist ?—in what part of us ?

SHARP. In the heart, I suppose, sir ?

EVE. Mr. Sharp, it exists in the breeches-pocket ! (*goes to table,* R.) Observe : I lay this piece of yellow earth on the table—I contemplate you both ; the man there—the gold here. Now, there is many a man in those streets honest as you are, who moves, thinks, feels, and reasons as well as we do ; excellent in form—imperishable in soul ; who, if his pockets were three days empty, would sell thought, reason, body, and soul, too, for that little coin ! Is that the fault of the man ?—no ! it is the fault of mankind ! God made man ; behold what mankind have made a god ! When I was poor, I hated the world ; now I am rich, I despise it ! Fools—knaves—hypocrites !—By the bye, Sharp, send £100 to the poor bricklayer whose house was burned down yesterday. (SHARP *goes to his desk.*)

Enter GRAVES, R.

Ah, Graves, my dear friend, what a world this is !

GRAVES. It is an atrocious world ! But astronomers say that there is a travelling comet which must set it on fire one day—and that's some comfort !

EVE. Every hour brings its gloomy lesson—the temper sours—the affections wither—the heart hardens into stone !—Zounds, Sharp ! what do you stand gaping there for ?—have you no bowels ?—why don't you go and see to the bricklayer ! (*to* SHARP, *who is standing* R. *Exit* SHARP, L.) Graves, of all my new friends—and their name is Legion—you are the only one I esteem ; there is sympathy between us—we take the same views of life. I am cordially glad to see you !

GRAVES (*groaning*). Ah ! why should you be glad to see a man so miserable ?

EVE (*sighs*). Because I am miserable myself.

GRAVES. You ! Pshaw ! *you* have not been condemned to lose a wife. (GRAVES *places his hat on table*, L.)

EVE. But, plague on it, man, I may be condemned to take one ! Sit down, and listen. (*they seat themselves*—GRAVES L) I want a confidant ! —Left fatherless when yet a boy, my poor mother grudged herself food to give me education. Some one had told her that learning was better than house and land—that's a lie, Graves !

GRAVES. A scandalous lie, Evelyn !

EVE. On the strength of that lie I was put to school—sent to college, a sizar. Do you know what a sizar is ? In pride he is a gentleman— in knowledge he is a scholar—and he crawls about, amidst gentlemen and scholars, with the livery of a pauper on his back ! I carried off the great prizes—I became distinguished—I looked to a high degree, leading to a fellowship ; that is, an independence for myself—a home for my mother. One day a young lord insulted me—I retorted—he struck me —refused apology—refused redress. I was a sizar !—a Pariah ! a thing —to *be* struck ! Sir, I was at least a man, and I horsewhipped him in the hall before the eyes of the whole College ! A few days, and the lord's chastisement was forgotten. The next day the sizar was expelled —the career of a life blasted ! That is the difference between Rich and Poor ; it takes a whirlwind to move the one—a breath may uproot the other ! I came to London. As long as my mother lived, I had one to toil for ; and I did toil—did hope—did struggle to be something yet. She died, and then, somehow, my spirit broke—I resigned myself to my fate ; the Alps above me seemed too high to ascend—I ceased to care what became of me. At last I submitted to be the poor relation—the hanger-on and gentleman-lackey of Sir John Vesey. But I had an object in that—there was one in that house whom I had loved at the first sight.

GRAVES And were you loved again ?

EVE. I fancied it, and was deceived. Not an hour before I inherited this mighty wealth I confessed my love, and was rejected because I was poor. Now, mark : you remember the letter which Sharp gave me when the will was read ?

GRAVES. Perfectly ! what were the contents ?

EVE. After hints, cautions, and admonitions—half in irony, half in earnest (Ah, poor Mordaunt had known the world !) it proceeded—but I'll read it to you : " Having selected you as my heir, because I think money a trust to be placed where it seems likely to be best employed, I now—not impose a condition, but ask a favor. If you have formed no other and insuperable attachment, I could wish to suggest your choice ;

my two nearest female relations are my niece Georgina, and my third cousin, Clara Douglas, the daughter of a once dear friend. If you could see in either of these one whom you could make your wife, such would be a marriage that, if I live long enough to return to England, I would seek to bring about before I die." My friend, this is not a legal condition—the fortune does not *rest* on it ; yet, need I say that my gratitude considers it a moral obligation? Several months have elapsed since thus called upon—I ought now to decide; you hear the names—Clara Douglas is the woman who rejected me.

GRAVES. But now she would accept you !

EVE. And do you think I am so base a slave to passion, that I would owe to my gold what was denied to my affection? (*rises and puts chair by* R. *table.*)

GRAVES. But you must choose one, in common gratitude ; you *ought* to do so. (GRAVES *replaces his chair.*)

EVE. Of the two, then, I would rather marry where I should exact the least. A marriage, to which each can bring sober esteem and calm regard, may not be happiness, but it may be content. But to marry one whom you could adore, and whose heart is closed to you—to yearn for the treasure, and only to claim the casket—to worship the statue that you never may warm to life. Oh! such a marriage would be a hell, the more terrible because Paradise was in sight. (*crosses to* R.)

GRAVES. Ah, it is a comfort to think, my dear friend, as you are sure to be miserable, when you are married, that we can mingle our groans together. Georgina is pretty, but vain and frivolous.

EVE. You may misjudge Georgina; she may have a nobler nature than appears on the surface. On the day, but before the hour, in which the will was read, a letter, in a strange or disguised hand, signed, " *From an unknown friend to Alfred Evelyn,*" and enclosing what to a girl would have been a considerable sum, was sent to a poor woman for whom I had implored charity, and whose address I had only given to Georgina.

GRAVES. Why not assure yourself?

EVE. Because I have not dared. For sometimes, against my reason, I have hoped that it might be Clara. (*taking a letter from his bosom and looking at it*) No, I can't recognize the hand. Graves, I detest that girl. (*crosses to* R. *corner and back to* L.)

GRAVES. Who? Georgina?

EVE. No; Clara! But I've already, thank Heaven, taken some revenge upon her. Come nearer. (*whispers*) I've bribed Sharp to say that Mordaunt's letter to me contained a codicil leaving Clara Douglas £20,000.

GRAVES. And didn't it?

EVE. Not a farthing. But I'm glad of it—I've paid the money—she's no more a dependant. No one can insult her now—she owes it all to me, and does not guess it, man—does not guess it—owes it to me—me, whom she rejected—me, the poor scholar! Ha! ha!—there's some spite in that, eh?

GRAVES. You're a fine fellow, Evelyn, and we understand each other. Perhaps Clara may have seen the address, and dictated this letter after all?

EVE. Do you think so—I'll go to the house this instant! (*crosses to* R. *table for his hat and gloves.*)

GRAVES. Eh! Humph! Then I'll go with you. That Lady Franklin is a fine woman. If she were not so gay, I think—I could——

EVE. No, no; don't think any such thing; women are even worse than men

GRAVES. True; to love is a boy's madness !

EVE. To feel is to suffer.

GRAVES. To hope is to be deceived.

EVE. I have done with romance !

GRAVES. Mine is buried with Maria !

EVE. If Clara did but write this——

GRAVES. Make haste, or Lady Franklin will be out ! (EVELYN *catches his eye ; he changes his tone*) A vale of tears—a vale of tears !

EVE. A vale of tears, indeed !   [*Exeunt,* R.

Re-enter GRAVES *for his hat.*

GRAVES. And I left my hat behind me ! Just like my luck. If I had been bred a hatter, little boys would have come into the world without heads.   [*Exit,* R.

SCENE II.—*Drawing-rooms at* SIR JOHN VESEY'S, *as in Act I., Scene I.*

LADY FRANKLIN *and* CLARA, R.

LADY F. (R.). Ha! ha! ha! talking of marriage, I've certainly made a conquest of Mr. Graves.

CLARA (L.). Mr. Graves ! I thought he was inconsolable.

LADY F. For his sainted Maria ! Poor man ! not contented with plaguing him while she lived, she must needs haunt him now she is dead.

CLARA. But why does he regret her ?

LADY F. Why ? Because he has everything to make him happy—easy fortune, good health, respectable character. And since it is his delight to be miserable, he takes the only excuse the world will allow him. For the rest—it's the way with widowers; that is, whenever they mean to marry again. But, my dear Clara, you seem absent—pale—unhappy—tears, too ?

CLARA. No—no—not tears. No !

LADY F. Ever since Mr. Mordaunt left you £20,000 every one admires you. Sir Frederick is desperately smitten.

CLARA (*with disdain*). Sir Frederick !

LADY F. Ah, Clara, be comforted ! I am certain that Evelyn loves you.

CLARA. If he did, it is past now. You alone know the true reason why I rejected him. You know that if ever he should learn that reason, he will acquit me of the selfish motive he now imputes to me.

Enter SIR JOHN, R.C., *and turns over the books, etc., on the table, as if to look for the newspaper.*

LADY F. Let me only tell him that you dictated that letter—that you sent that money to his old nurse. Poor Clara ! it was your little all. He will then know, at least, if avarice be your sin.

CLARA. He would have guessed it had *his* love been like *mine.*

LADY F. Guessed it—nonsense ! The hand-writing unknown to him—every reason to think it came from Georgina.

SIR J. (*aside,* R., *at table*). Hum ! Came from Georgina.

LADY F. Come, *let* me tell him *this.* I know the effect it will have upon his choice.

CLARA. Choice ! oh, that humiliating word. No, Lady Franklin, no ! Promise me !

LADY F. But——

CLARA. No ! Promise—faithfully—sacredly.

LADY F. Well, I promise.

CLARA. I—I—forgive me—I am not well.   [*Exit, R.*

LADY F. What fools these girls are!—they take as much pains to lose
a husband as a poor widow does to get one!

SIR J. Have you seen "The Times" newspaper? Where the deuce is
the newspaper? I can't find "The Times" newspaper.

LADY F. I think it is in my room. Shall I fetch it?

SIR J. My dear sister—you're the best creature. Do!

[*Exit LADY FRANKLIN, R.*

Ugh! you unnatural conspirator against your own family! What can
this *letter* be? Ah! I recollect something.

Enter GEORGINA, R. C.

GEOR. (L.). Papa, I want—

SIR J. Yes, I know what you want well enough! Tell me!—were
you aware that Clara had sent money to that old nurse Evelyn bored us
about the day of the will?

GEOR. No! He gave me the address, and I promised, if——

SIR J. Gave you *the address?*—that's lucky! Hush!

Enter PAGE, C. L.

PAGE (*announces*). Mr. Graves—Mr. Evelyn.   [*Exit, C. L.*

Enter GRAVES *and* EVELYN, C. L. EVELYN, *when he enters, goes to* SIR
JOHN, *then converses with* GEORGINA, *who is seated* R. *of* L. *table.*

LADY F. (*returning*). Here is the newspaper.

GRAVES. Ay—read the newspapers!—they'll tell you what this world
is made of. Daily calendars of roguery and woe! Here, advertise-
ments from quacks, money-lenders, cheap warehouses, and spotted boys
with two heads. So much for dupes and impostors! Turn to the other
column—police reports, bankruptcies, swindling, forgery, and a bio-
graphical sketch of the snub-nosed man who murdered his own three
little cherubs at Pentonville. Do you fancy these but exceptions to the
general virtue and health of the nation?—Turn to the leading articles;
and your hair will stand on end at the horrible wickedness or melancholy idiotism of that half of the population who think differently from
yourself. In my day I have seen already eighteen crises, six annihi-
lations of Agriculture and Commerce, four overthrows of the Church,
and three last, final, awful, and irremediable destructions of the entire
Constitution. And that's a newspaper!

LADY F. (R. C.). Ha! ha! your usual vein; always so amusing and
good-humored!

GRAVES (L. C., *frowning and very angry*). Ma'am—good-humored!

LADY F. Ah, you should always wear that agreeable smile; you look
so much younger—so much handsomer—when you smile!

GRAVES (*softened*). Ma'am—(*aside*) A charming creature, upon my
word!

LADY F. You have not seen the last *Punch?* It is excellent. I think
it might make you *laugh.* But, by the bye, I don't think you can laugh.

GRAVES. Ma'am—I have not laughed since the death of my sainted
Ma——

LADY F. Ah! and that spiteful Sir Frederick says you never laugh,
because—But you'll be angry?

GRAVES. Angry!—pooh! I despise Sir Frederick too much to let anything he says have the smallest influence over me! He says I don't laugh, because——

LADY F. You have lost your front teeth.

GRAVES. Lost my front teeth! Upon my word! Ha! ha! ha! That's too good—capital! Ha! ha! ha! (*laughing from ear to ear.*)

LADY F. Ha! ha! ha! [*Exeunt* LADY FRANKLIN *and* GRAVES, C.

EVE. (*aside, at* R. *table*). Of course Clara will not appear! avoids me as usual! But what do I care?—what is she to me? Nothing!

SIR J. (*to* GEORGINA). Yes—yes—leave me to manage; you took his portrait, as I told you?

GEOR. Yes—but I could not catch the expression. I got Clara to touch it up.

SIR J. That girl's always in the way. (PAGE *from* C. L. *announces* CAP-TAIN DUDLEY SMOOTH.)

Enter CAPTAIN DUDLEY SMOOTH, C. L.

SMOOTH. Good morning, dear John. Ah, Miss Vesey, you have no idea of the conquests you made at Almack's last night.

EVE. (*examining him curiously while* SMOOTH *is talking to* GEORGINA *at* L. *table*). And that's the celebrated Dudley Smooth!

SIR J. (R. C.). More commonly called Deadly Smooth!—the finest player at whist, écarté, billiards, chess, and picquet, between this and the Pyramids—the sweetest manners!—always calls you by your Christian name. But take care how you play at cards with him!

EVE. He does not cheat, I suppose?

SIR J. Hist! *No!*—but he always *wins!* He's an uncommonly clever fellow!

EVE. Clever? yes! When a man steals a loaf we cry down the knavery—when a man diverts his neighbor's mill-stream to grind his own corn, we cry up the cleverness! And every one courts Captain Dudley Smooth?

SIR J. Why, who could offend him?—the best-bred, civilest creature —and a dead shot! There is not a cleverer man in the three kingdoms.

EVE. A study—a study!—let me examine him! Such men are living satires on the world. (*rises.*)

SMOOTH (*passing his arm caressingly over* SIR JOHN'S *shoulder*). My dear John, how well you are looking! A new lease of life! Introduce me to Mr. Evelyn.

EVE. Sir, it's an honor I've long ardently desired. (*crossses to him— they bow and shake hands.* PAGE *announces* SIR FREDERICK BLOUNT.)

Enter SIR FREDERICK BLOUNT, C. L.

BLOUNT. How d'ye do, Sir John? Ah, Evelyn—I wished so much to see you. (*takes* EVELYN'S *arm and draws him towards* L. C.)

EVE. 'Tis my misfortune to be visible!

BLOUNT. A little this way. You know, perhaps, that I once paid my addwesses to Miss Vesey; but since that vewy eccentwic will Sir John has shuffled me off, and hints at a pwior attachment—(*aside*) which I know to be false.

EVE. (*seeing* CLARA). A prior attachment!—Ha! Clara! Well, an-other time, my dear Blount.

Enter CLARA, R. *She seats herself* L. *of* R. *table.*

BLOUNT. Stay a moment. Why are you in such a howwid huwwy?
I want you to do me a favor with regard to Miss Douglas.

EVE. Miss Douglas!

BLOUNT. It is whispered about that you mean to pwopose to Georgina. Nay, Sir John more than hinted that was her pwior attachment!

EVE. Indeed!

BLOUNT. Yes. Now, as you are all in all with the family, if you could say a word for me to Miss Douglas, I don't see what harm it could do me!

EVE. 'Sdeath, man! speak for yourself! you are just the sort of man for young ladies to like—they understand you—you're of their own level. Pshaw! you're too modest—you want no mediator!

BLOUNT. My dear fellow, you flatter me. I'm well enough in my way. But you, you know, would cawwy evewything before you—you're so confoundedly wich!

EVE. You really think so, and you wish me to say a word for you to Miss Douglas? (*he takes* BLOUNT'S *arm and walks him to* CLARA) Miss Douglas, what do you think of Sir Frederick Blount? Observe him. He is well dressed—young—tolerably handsome—(BLOUNT *bowing*) bows with an air—has plenty of small talk—everything to captivate. Yet he thinks that, if he and I were suitors to the same lady, I should be more successful because I am richer. What say you? Is love an auction?—and *do* women's hearts go to the highest bidder?

CLARA. Their hearts—no!

EVE. But their hands—yes! (*she turns away*) You turn away. Ah, you dare not answer that question! (BLOUNT *crosses to* CLARA, SMOOTH *and* SIR JOHN *go up the stage;* EVELYN *goes to* GEORGINA, *at* L. *table.*)

BLOUNT. I wish you would take my opewa-box next Saturday—'tis the best in the house. I'm not wich, but I spend what I have on myself. I make it a wule to have everything of the best in a quiet way. Best opewa-box—best dogs—best horses—best house in town of its kind. I want nothing to complete my establishment but the best wife.

CLARA. Oh, that will come in time.

GEOR. (*aside*). Sir Frederick flirting with Clara? I'll punish him for his perfidy. (*aloud*) *You* are the last person to talk so, Mr. Evelyn—you, whose wealth is your smallest attraction—you, whom every one admires—so witty, such taste, such talent! Ah, I'm very foolish.

SIR J. (*clapping* EVELYN *on the shoulder*). You must not turn my little girl's head. Oh, you're a sad fellow! Apropos, I must show you Georgina's last drawings. She's wonderfully improved since you gave her lessons in perspective.

GEOR. No, papa! No, pray, no! Nay, don't!

SIR J. Nonsense, child—it's very odd, but she's more afraid of you than of any one! (*goes to the folio stand.*)

SMOOTH (*aside*). He's an excellent father, our dear John! and supplies the place of a mother to her. (*lounges off,* C.)

CLARA (*aside*). So, so—he loves her! Misery—misery! But he shall not perceive it. No, no! (*aloud*) Ha, ha! Sir Frederick—excellent! excellent! You are so entertaining. (SIR JOHN *brings a portfolio and places it on the table;* EVELYN *and* GEORGINA *look over the drawings;* SIR JOHN *leans over them;* SIR FREDERICK *converses with* CLARA; EVELYN *watching them.*)

EVE. Beautiful!—a view from Tivoli. (Death—she looks down while he speaks to her!) Is there a little fault in that coloring? (she positively blushes) But this Jupiter is superb. (What a d—d cocoxcomb it is?) (*rising*) Oh, she certainly loves him—I too, can be loved elsewhere—I, too, can see smiles and blushes on the face of another.

GEOR. Are you not well? (*going to him*, L. C.)

EVE. I beg pardon. Yes you are indeed improved. Ah, who so accomplished as Miss Vesey? (*re es with her to the table; taking up a portrait*) Why, what is this?—my own——

GEOR. You must not look at that—you must not, indeed. I did not know it was there.

SIR J. Your own portrait, Evelyn! Why, child, I was not aware you took likenesses—that's something new. Upon my word it's a strong resemblance.

GEOR. Oh, no—it does not do him justice. Give it to me. I will tear it. (*aside*) That odious Sir Frederick!

EVE. Nay you shall not. (CLARA *looks at him reproachfully, then talks with* SIR FREDERICK) But where is the new guitar you meant to buy, Miss Vesey—the one inlaid with tortoise shell? It it nearly a year since you set your heart on it, and I don't see it yet.

SIR J. (R. C., *taking him aside, confidentially*) The guitar—oh, to tell you a secret—she applied the money I gave her for it to a case of charity several months ago—the very day the will was read. I saw the letter lying on the table, with the money in it. Mind, not a word to her—she'd never forgive me.

EVE. Letter—money! What was the name of the person she relieved—not Stanton?

SIR J. I don't remember, indeed.

EVE. (*taking out letter*). This is not her hand!

SIR J. No! I observed at the time it was not her hand, but I got out from her that she did not wish the thing to *be known*, and had employed some one else to copy it. May I see the letter? Yes, I think this is the wording. Still, how did she know Mrs. Stanton's address?

EVE. I gave it to her, Sir John.

CLARA (*at the distance*). Yes, I'll go to the opera, if Lady Franklin will—on Saturday, then, Sir Frederick. (BLOUNT *bows to* CLARA *and goes off*, C. L.)

EVE. Sir John, to a man like me, this simple act of unostentatious generosity is worth all the accomplishments in the world. A good heart—a tender disposition—a charity that shuns the day—a modesty that blushes at its own excellence—an impulse towards something more divine than Mammon; such are the true accomplishments which preserve beauty for ever young. Such I have sought in the partner I would take for life—such have I found—alas! not where I had dreamed! Miss Vesey, I will be honest. (MISS VESEY *advances*, L. H.) I say then, frankly—(*raising his voice, as* CLARA *approaches, and looking fixedly at her*)—I have loved another—deeply—truly—bitterly—*vainly!* I cannot offer to you, as I did to her, the fair first love of the human heart—rich with all its blossoms and its verdure. But if esteem—if gratitude—if an earnest resolve to conquer every recollection that would wander from your image; if these can tempt you to accept my hand and fortune, my life shall be a study to deserve your confidence. (*during this speech* GEORGINA *has advanced*, L., CLARA *to a chair* R. *of* L. *table;* CLARA *sits motionless, clasping her hands.*)

SIR J. The happiest day of my life. (CLARA *falls back in her chair.*)

EVE. (*darting forward, aside*). She is pale; she faints. What have I done? Oh, Heaven! (*aloud*) Clara!

CLARA (*rising with a smile*). Be happy, my cousin—be happy! Yes, with my whole heart I say it—be happy, Alfred Evelyn! (*she sinks again into the chair, overcome by emotion; the rest form a picture of consternation and selfish joy.*)

CURTAIN.

ACT III.

SCENE I.—*The drawing-rooms in* SIR JOHN VESEY's *house, as before. The furniture arranged for the change to the next scene.*

SIR JOHN *and* GEORGINA *discovered,* C.

SIR J. And he has not pressed you to fix the wedding-day?

GEOR. No; and since he proposed he comes here so seldom, and seems so gloomy. Heigho! Poor Sir Frederick was twenty times more amusing.

SIR J. But Evelyn is fifty times as rich.

GEOR. But do you not fear lest he discover that Clara wrote the letter?

SIR J. No; and I shall get Clara out of the house. But there is something else that makes me very uneasy. You know that no sooner did Evelyn come into possession of his fortune than he launched out in the style of a prince. His house in London is a palace, and he has bought a great estate in the country. Look how he lives. Balls—banquets—fine arts—fiddlers—charities—and the devil to pay!

GEOR. But if he can afford it——

SIR J. Oh! so long as he stopped *there* I had no apprehension; but since he proposed for you he is more extravagant than ever. They say he has taken to gambling; and he is always with Captain Smooth. No fortune can stand Deadly Smooth! If he gets into a scrape he may fall off from the settlements. We must press the marriage at once.

GEOR. Heigho! Poor Frederick! You don't think he is *really* attached to Clara?

SIR J. Upon my word I can't say. Put on your bonnet, and come to Storr and Mortimer's to choose the jewels.

GEOR. The jewels—yes—the drive will do me good.

SIR J. Tell Clara to come to me. (*exit* GEORGINA, R.) Yes. I must press on this marriage. Georgina has not wit enough to manage him—at least till he's her husband, and then all women find it smooth sailing. This match will make me a man of prodigious importance! I suspect he'll give me up her ten thousand pounds. I can't think of his taking to gambling, for I love him as a son—and I look on his money as my own.

Enter CLARA, R.

SIR J. Clara, my love!

CLARA. Sir——

SIR J. My dear, what I am going to say may appear a little rude and unkind, but you know my character is frankness. To the point then; my poor child, I am aware of your attachment to Mr. Evelyn——

CLARA. Sir! *my attachment?*

SIR J. It is generally remarked. Lady Kind says you are falling away. My poor girl, I pity you—I do, indeed. (CLARA *weeps*) My dear Clara, don't take on so; I would not have said this for the world, if I was not a little anxious about my own girl. Georgina is so unhappy at what every one says of your attachment——

CLARA. Every one? Oh, torture!

SIR J. That it preys on her spirits—it even irritates her temper! In a word, I fear these little jealousies and suspicions will tend to embitter their future union. I'm a father—forgive me.

CLARA. What would you have me do, sir?

SIR J. Why, you're now independent. Lady Franklin seems resolved to stay in town. You are your own mistress. Mrs. Carlton, aunt to my late wife, is going abroad for a short time, and would be delighted if you would accompany her.

CLARA. It is the very favor I would have asked of you. (*aside*) I shall escape at least the struggle and the shame. (*aloud*) When does she go ?

SIR J. In five days—next Monday.—You forgive me ?

CLARA. Sir, I thank you.

SIR J. Suppose, then, you write a line to her yourself, and settle it at once ?

Takes CLARA *to table,* L., *as the* PAGE *enters* C. L.

PAGE. The carriage, Sir John ; Miss Vesey is quite ready.

SIR J. Very well, James. If Mr. Serious, the clergyman, calls, say I'm gone to the great meeting at Exeter Hall; if Lord Spruce calls, say you believe I'm gone to the rehearsal of Cinderella. Oh ! and if Mac-Finch should come (MacFinch who duns me three times a week), say I've hurried off to Garraway's to bid for the great Bulstrode estate. Just put the Duke of Lofty's card carelessly on the hall table. (*exit* SERVANT, R. C.) One must have a little management in this world. All humbug !—all humbug, upon my soul !   [*Exit,* C. L.

CLARA (*folding the letter*). There, it is decided ! A few days, and we are parted for ever !—a few weeks, and another will bear his name—his wife ! Oh, happy fate ! She will have the right to say to him—though the whole world should hear her—" I am thine !" And I embitter their lot ! And yet, O Alfred ! if she loves thee—if she knows thee—if she values thee—and, when thou wrong'st her, if she can forgive, as I do—I can bless her when far away, and join her name in my prayer for thee !

EVE. (*without*). Miss Vesey just gone ! Well, I will write a line.

Enter EVELYN, C. L., *preceded by* PAGE, *who exits immediately,* C. L.

EVE. (*aside*). So—Clara ! (*she rises, crosses to* R.) Do not let me disturb you, Miss Douglas.

CLARA (*going,* R.). Nay, I have done.

EVE. I see that my presence is always odious to you ; it is a reason why I come so seldom. But be cheered, madam ; I am here but to fix the day of my marriage. and I shall then go into the country—till—till —In short, this is the last time my visit will banish you from the room I enter. (*he places his hat on table,* L.)

CLARA (*aside*). The last time !—and we shall then meet no more ! And to thus part forever—in scorn—in anger—I cannot bear it ! (*approaches him*) Alfred, my cousin, it is true, this may be the last time we shall meet—I have made my arrangements to quit England.

EVE. To quit England ? (*comes forward,* L.)

CLARA. But before I go let me thank you for many a past kindness, which it is not for an orphan easily to forget.

EVE (*mechanically*). To quit England ?

CLARA. Yes, and now that you are betrothed to another—now, without recurring to the past—something of our old friendship may at least return to us And if, too, I dared, I have that on my mind which only a friend—a sister—might presume to say to you.

EVE. (*moved*). Miss Douglas—Clara—if there is aught that I could do —if, while hundreds—strangers—beggars tell me that I have the power, by opening or shutting this worthless hand, to bid sorrow rejoice, or poverty despair—if—if my life—my heart's blood—could render to *you* one such service as my gold can give to others—why, speak !—and the past you allude to—yes, even that bitter past—I will cancel and forget.

CLARA (*holding out her hand*). We are friends, then! (EVELYN *takes her hand*) You are again my cousin!—my brother!

EVE. (*dropping her hand*). Brother! Ah! say on!

CLARA. I speak, then, as a sister—herself weak, inexperienced—*might* speak to a brother, in whose career she felt the ambition of a man. On! Evelyn, when you inherited this vast wealth I pleased myself with imagining how you would wield the power delegated to your hands. I knew your benevolence—your intellect—your genius! I saw before me the noble and bright career open to you at last—and I often thought that, in after years, when far away—as I soon shall be—I should hear your name identified, not with what fortune can give the base, but with deeds and ends to which, for the *great*, fortune is but the instrument;—I often thought that I should say to my own heart—weeping proud and delicious tears—"And once this man loved me!"

EVE. No more, Clara!—Oh, heavens!—no more!

CLARA. But *has* it been so?—have you been true to your own self?—Pomp—parade—luxuries—pleasures—follies!—all these might distinguish others—they do but belie the ambition and the soul of Alfred Evelyn. Oh! pardon me—I am too bold—I pain—I offend you.—Ah! I should not have dared thus much had I not thought at times, that—that——

EVE. That these follies—these vanities—this dalliance with a loftier fate were your own work! You thought that, and you were right! Perhaps, indeed, after a youth, steeped to the lips in the hyssop and gall of penury—perhaps I might have wished royally to know the full value of that dazzling and starry life which, from the last step in the ladder, I had seen indignantly and from afar. But a month—a week, would have sufficed for that experience. Experience!—Oh, how soon we learn that hearts are as cold and souls as vile—no matter whether the sun shine on the noble in his palace, or the rain drench the rags of the beggar cowering at the porch. But you—did not you reject me because I was poor? Despise me, if you please!—my revenge might be unworthy—I wished to show you the luxuries, the gaud, the splendor I thought you prized—to surround with the attributes your sex seems most to value—the station that, had you loved me, it would have been yours to command. But vain—vain alike my poverty and my wealth! You loved me not in either, and my fate is sealed!

CLARA. A happy fate, Evelyn!—you love!

EVE. And at last I am beloved. (*after a pause, and turning to her abruptly*) Do you doubt it?

CLARA. No, I believe it firmly!—And, now that there is nothing unkind between us—not even regret—and surely (*with a smile*) not revenge, my cousin, you will rise to your nobler self!—and so, farewell! (*going*, R)

EVE. No; stay, one moment;—you still feel interest in my fate? Have I been deceived? Oh, why—why did you spurn the heart whose offerings were lavished at your feet? Could you still—still——? Distraction—I know not what I say;—my honor pledged to another—my vows accepted and returned! Go, Clara, it is best so! Yet you will miss some one, perhaps, more than me—some one to whose follies you have been more indulgent—some one to whom you would permit a yet tenderer name than that of brother! (*goes to table*, L.)

CLARA (*aside*). It will make him, perhaps, happier to think it! (*aloud*) Think so, if you will!—but part friends.

EVE. Friends—and that is all! Look you—this is life! The eyes that charmed away every sorrow—the hand whose lightest touch thrilled to the very core—the voice that, heard afar, filled space as with an angel's music—a year—a month, a day, and we smile that we could dream so idly. All—all—the sweetest enchantment, known but once, never to return again, vanished from the world! And the one who forgets the soonest—the one who robs your earth for ever of its sunshine—comes to you with a careless lip, and says—"Let us part friends!"—Go, Clara—go—and be happy if you can! (*falls into a chair at* L. *table*.)

CLARA (*weeping*). Cruel—cruel—to the last!   [*Exit*, R.

EVE. (*rises*). Soft! let me recall her words, her tones, her looks.—*Does she love me?* There is a voice at my heart which tells me I have been the rash slave of a jealous anger. But I have made my choice—I must abide the issue. (*retires and sits at* R. *table*.)

Enter GRAVES, *preceded by* PAGE, L. C.

PAGE. Lady Franklin is dressing, sir.

GRAVES. Well, I'll wait. (*exit* PAGE, R.) She was worthy to have known the lost Maria! So considerate to ask me hither—not to console me, *that* is impossible—but to indulge the luxury of woe. It will be a mournful scene. (*seeing* EVELYN) Is that you, Evelyn? I have just heard that the borough of Broginhole is vacant at last. Why not stand yourself—with your property you might come in without even a personal canvass.

EVE. I, who despise these contests for the color of a straw. (*aside*) And yet, Clara spoke of ambition. She would regret me if I could be distinguished. (*rises, aloud*) You are right, Graves, to be sure, after all. An Englishman owes something to his country.

GRAVES (L.). He does, indeed. (*counting on his fingers*) East winds, Fogs, Rheumatism, Pulmonary Complaints, and Taxes. (EVELYN *walks about in disorder*) Oh! you are a pretty fellow. One morning you tell me you love Clara, or at least detest her, which is the same thing (poor Maria often said she detested *me*), and that very afternoon you propose to Georgina.

EVE. Clara will easily console herself—thanks to Sir Frederick!

GRAVES. Nevertheless, Clara has had the bad taste to refuse an offer from Sir Frederick. I have it from Lady Franklin, to whom he confided his despair in re-arranging his neck-cloth.

EVE. My dear friend—is it possible?

GRAVES. But what then? You *must* marry Georgina, who, to believe Lady Franklin, is sincerely attached to—your fortune. Go and hang yourself, Evelyn; you have been duped by them.

EVE. By them—bah! If deceived, I have been my own dupe. Is it not a strange thing that in matters of reason—of the arithmetic and logic of life—we are sensible, shrewd, prudent men; but touch our hearts—move our passions—take us for an instant from the hard safety of worldly calculation—and the philosopher is duller than the fool? (*crosses*, L.) *Duped*—if I thought it—but Georgina?

GRAVES. Plays affection to you in the afternoon, after practising with Sir Frederick in the morning.

EVE. On your life, sir, be serious; what do you mean?

GRAVES. That in passing this way I see her very often walking in the square with Sir Frederick.

EVE. Ha! say you so?

GRAVES. What then? Man is born to be deceived. You look nervous—your hand trembles; that comes of gaming. They say at the clubs that you play deeply.

EVE. Ha! ha! Do they say that? a few hundreds lost or won—a cheap opiate—anything that can lay the memory to sleep. The poor

man drinks, and the rich man gambles—the same motive to both.   But
you are right—it is a base resource—I will play no more.

GRAVES. I am delighted to hear it, for your friend Captain Smooth
has ruined half the young heirs in London.   Even Sir John is alarmed.
I met him just now in Pall Mall.   By-the-bye, I forgot—do you bank
with Flash, Brisk, Credit and Co. ?

EVE. So, Sir John is alarmed. (*aside*) Gulled by this cogging charla-
tan?   Aha! I may beat him yet at his own weapons. (*aloud*) Humph!
Bank with Flash!   Why do you ask me ?

GRAVES. Because Sir John has just heard that they are in a very bad
way, and begs you to withdraw anything you have in their hands.

EVE. I'll see to it.   So Sir John is *alarmed* at my gambling?

GRAVES. Terribly!   He even told me he should go himself to the
club this evening, to watch you.

EVE. To watch me—good—I will be there !

GRAVES. But you will promise not to play ?

EVE. Yes—to play.   I feel it is impossible to give it up.

GRAVES. No—no !   'Sdeath, man ! be as wretched as you please ;
break your heart, that's nothing ! but damme, take care of your pockets.

EVE. Hark ye, Graves—if you are right, I will extricate myself yet.
The duper shall be duped, in the next twenty-four hours.   I may win
back the happiness of a life.   Oh ! if this scheme do but succeed !

GRAVES. Scheme !   What scheme ? (EVELYN *takes his hat from* L.
table.)

EVE. Yes, I will be there—I will play with Captain Smooth—I will
lose as much as I please—thousands—millions—billions ; and if he presume to spy on my losses, hang me, if I don't lose Sir John himself into
the bargain ! (*going out and returning*) I am so absent.   What was the
bank you mentioned ?   Flash, Brisk and Credit !   Bless me, how unlucky ! and it's too late to draw out to-day.   Tell Sir John I'm very
much obliged to him, and he'll find me at the club any time before day-
break, hard at work with my friend Smooth.   [*Exit*, C. L.

GRAVES. He's certainly crazy ! but I don't wonder at it.   What the
approach of the dog-days is to the canine species, the approach of the
honeymoon is to the human race.

Enter SERVANT, R.

SER. Lady Franklin's compliments—she will see you in the *boudoir*,
sir.

GRAVES. In the *boudoir !*—go—go—I'll come directly. (*exit* SERVANT,
R.) My heart beats—it must be for grief.   Poor Maria ! (*searching his
pockets for his handkerchief*) Not a white one—just like my luck ; I call
on a lady to talk of the dear departed, and I've nothing about me but a
cursed gaudy, flaunting, red, yellow and blue abomination from India,
which it's even indecent for a disconsolate widower to exhibit.   Ah !
Fortune never ceases to torment the susceptible.   The *boudoir*—ha—ha !
the *boudoir !*   [*Exit*, R.

SCENE II.—*A boudoir in the same house.   Two chairs brought on by a*
PAGE, *who goes off,* L.

Enter LADY FRANKLIN, L.

LADY F. What if my little plot does not succeed ?   The man insists
on being wretched, and I pity him so much that I am determined to

make him happy! Ha! ha! ha! He shall laugh, he shall sing, he
shall dance, he shall—(*composes herself*) Here he comes!

Enter GRAVES, R.

GRAVES (*sighing*). Ah, Lady Franklin!

LADY F. (*sighing*). Ah, Mr. Graves! (*they seat themselves*) Pray excuse
me for having kept you so long. Is it not a charming day?

GRAVES. An east wind, ma'am! but nothing comes amiss to you—'tis
a happy disposition! Poor Maria! she, too, was naturally gay.

LADY F. Yes, she was gay. So much life, and a great deal of spirit.

GRAVES. Spirit? Yes—nothing could master it! She *would* have
her own way. Ah! there was nobody like her!

LADY F. And then, when her spirit was up, she looked so handsome!
Her eyes grew so brilliant!

GRAVES. Did not they?—Ah! ah! ha! ha! ha! And do you remember her pretty trick of stamping her foot?—the tiniest little foot—
I think I see her now. Ah! this conversation is very soothing!

LADY F. How well she acted in your private theatricals!

GRAVES. You remember her Mrs. Oakley, in "The Jealous Wife?"
Ha! ha! how good it was!—ha! ha!

LADY F. Ha! ha! Yes, in the very first scene, when she came out
with (*mimicking*) "Your unkindness and barbarity will be the death of
me!"

GRAVES. No—no! that's not it! more energy. (*mimicking*) "Your
unkindness and barbarity will be the DEATH of me!" Ha! ha! I ought
to know how she said it, for she used to practice it on me twice a day.
Ah! poor dear lamb! (*wipes his eyes.*)

LADY F. And then she sang so well! was such a composer! What
was that little air she was so fond of?

GRAVES. Ha! ha! sprightly, was it not? Let me see—let me see.

LADY F. (*humming*). Tum ti—ti tum—ti—ti—ti. No. that's not it!

GRAVES (*humming*). Tum ti—ti—tum ti—ti—tum—tum—tum.

BOTH. Tum ti—ti—tum ti—ti—tum—tum—tum. Ha! ha!

GRAVES (*throwing himself back*). Ah! what recollection it revives! It
is too affecting.

LADY F. It *is* affecting; but we are all mortal. (*sighs*) And at your
Christmas party at Cyprus Lodge, do you remember her dancing the
Scotch reel with Captain MacNaughten?

GRAVES. Ha! ha! ha! To be sure—to be sure.

LADY F. Can you think of the step?—somehow thus, was it not?
(*dancing.*)

GRAVES. No—no—quite wrong!—just stand there. Now then—
(*humming the tune*) La—la-la-la—La-la, etc. (*they dance*) That's it—excellent—admirable!

LADY F. (*aside*). Now 'tis coming.

Enter SIR JOHN, BLOUNT, GEORGINA, R. *They stand amazed.* LADY
FRANKLIN *continues dancing.*

GRAVES. Bewitching—irresistible! 'Tis Maria herself that I see before me! Thus—thus—let me clasp——Oh, the devil! Just like my
luck! (*stopping opposite* SIR JOHN. LADY FRANKLIN *runs off*, L.)

SIR J. Upon *my* word, Mr. Graves!

GEOR. *and* BLOUNT. Encore—encore! Bravo—bravo!

GRAVES. It's all a mistake! I—I—Sir John. Lady Franklin, you see—that is to say—I——Sainted Maria! you are spared, at least, this affliction!   [*Runs off*, R.

SIR JOHN, GEORGINA, *and* BLOUNT *follow*.   PAGE *takes off the chairs*, L.

SCENE III.—*The interior of* * * * *'*s Club ; night ; lights, etc., etc.**

Noise of conversation before the act-drop rises—murmurs as it ascends.

GLOSS. You don't often come to the Club, Stout?

STOUT. No; time is money.   An hour spent at a club is unproductive capital.

OLD MEMBER (*reading the newspaper*). Waiter! the snuff-box. (WAITER *brings a large round box on a salver.*)

GLOSS. So, Evelyn has taken to play?   I see Deadly Smooth, "hushed in grim repose, awaits his evening prey."   Deep work to-night, I suspect, for Smooth is drinking lemonade—keeps his head clear—monstrous clever dog! (*murmurs as before ;* STOUT *takes the snuff-box from* OLD MEMBER'S *table ;* OLD MEMBER *looks at him savagely.*)

Enter EVELYN; *salutes and shakes hands with different* MEMBERS *in passing up the stage ; places his hat on table,* C.

EVE. Ha, Flat, how well you are looking!—Green, how do you do? How d'ye do, Glossmore?   How are you, Stout? *you* don't play, I think?   Political Economy never plays at cards, eh?—never has time for anything more frivolous than Rents and Profits, Wages and Labor, High Prices, and Low—Corn-Laws, Poor-Laws, Tithes, Currency,—Dot-and-go-one—Rates, Puzzles, Taxes, Riddles, and Botheration!   Smooth is the man.   Aha! Smooth.   Piquet, eh?   You owe me my revenge! (*sits to play,* L. *of* R. *table ;* MEMBERS *touch each other significantly.*)

SMOOTH. My dear Alfred, anything to oblige. (*murmurs.*)

OLD MEM. Waiter! the snuff-box. (WAITER *takes it from* STOUT *and brings it back to* OLD MEMBER.   *Two* MEMBERS *from the top,* L., *come down and cross behind to* MEMBER R. *of centre table, whisper to him and go off,* C. WAITER *brings coffee to* MEMBER *behind the* OLD MEMBER, *and then takes away two coffee cups from* LORD GLOSSMORE *and* MEMBER, R. C.   *Another* WAITER *brings a glass of brandy and water to* OLD MEMBER.   *Having made the cards,* SMOOTH *deals.*)

Enter BLOUNT, C.; *he goes to* EVELYN's *table, and stands in front of it for a moment.*

BLOUNT. So!   Evelyn at it again—eh, Glossmore?

GLOSS. Yes; Smooth sticks to him like a leech.   Clever fellow, that Smooth. (*murmurs.*   SMOOTH *and* EVELYN *play.*)

SMOOTH. Your point?

EVE. Five!

SMOOTH. Not good.   Six—sequence—five!

EVE. Good!

SMOOTH. Three aces.

EVE. Good! (*they continue playing ;* EVELYN *deals.*)

BLOUNT. Will you make up a wubber?

GLOSS. Have you got two others?

BLOUNT. Yes; Flat and Green.

---

* For full disposition of this scene and characters as discovered, see the Synopsis of Scenery, page 3.

Gloss. Bad players.

Blount. I make it a wule to play with bad players; it is five per cent. in one's favor. I hate gambling. But a quiet wubber, if one is the best player out of four, can't do any harm.

Gloss. Clever fellow, that Blount. (*murmurs*. Blount *takes up the snuff-box and walks off with it;* Old Member *looks at him savagely.* Waiter *fetches coffee-cup from* Member, L.)

Enter a Member *reading a long letter ; sits, c. table.* Blount, Glossmore, Flat, *and* Green, *make up a table at the bottom of the stage,* R.

Smooth. A thousand pardons, my dear Alfred—ninety repique—ten cards—game !

Eve. (*passing a note to him*). Game ! Before we go on, one qnestion. This is Thursday—how much do you calculate to win of me before Tuesday next?

Smooth. *Ce cher Alfred !* He is so droll !

Eve. (*writing in his pocket-book*). Forty games a night—four nights, minus Sunday—our usual stakes—that would be right, I think.

Smooth (*glancing over the account*). Quite —if I win all—which is next to impossible.

Eve. It shall be possible to win twice as much, on one condition. Can you keep a secret?

Smooth. My dear Alfred, I have kept myself ! I never inherited a farthing—I never spent less than £4,000 a year—and I never told a soul how I managed it.

Eve. Hark ye, then—it is a matter to me of vast importance—a word with you. (*they whisper.*)

Old Mem. Waiter ! the snuff-box. (Waiter *takes it from* Blount, *etc. Murmurs.*)

Enter Sir John, c.

Eve. You understand ?

Smooth. Perfectly ; anything to oblige.

Eve. (*cutting*). It is for you to deal. (*murmurs.   They go on playing.*)

Waiter *comes on with a note, on salver, and offers it to one of the* Members, *who is looking on at the whist-table : he scribbles an answer, at* c. *table, and sends the* Waiter *off with it.*

Sir J. There is my precious son-in-law, that is to be, spending *my* consequence, and making a fool of himself. (*takes up snuff-box ;* Old Member *looks at him.*)

Eve (*playing*). Six to the point.

Smooth. Good !

Eve. Three queens.

Smooth. Not good—I have three kings and three knaves ! (*they deal out the cards until* Sir John *speaks.*)

Blount (*rising from the table ; another* Member *takes his place*). I'm out. Flat, a pony on the odd twick. (*takes the money*) That's wight. (*comes down,* R. c., *counting money*) Well, Sir John, you don't play !

Sir J. Play? no! (*looking over* Evelyn's *hand*) Confound him—lost again !

Eve. Hang the cards!—double the stakes !

Smooth. Anything to oblige—done !

Sir J. Done, indeed !

Old Mem. Waiter ! the snuff-box. (Waiter *takes it from* Sir John.)

Blount. I've won eight points and the bets—I never lose—I never play in the Deadly Smooth set! (*takes up the snuff-box ;* OLD MEMBER *as before.*)

SIR J. (*looking over* SMOOTH's *hand, and fidgeting backwards and forwards*). Lord, have mercy on us! Smooth has seven for his point! What's the stakes?

EVE. Don't disturb us—I only throw out four. Stakes, Sir John?—immense! Was ever such luck?—not a card for my point. Do stand back, Sir John—I'm getting irritable. (*all rise and gather round* EVELYN's *table ; several in front, so as to hide the playing from the audience.*)

BLOUNT. One hundred pounds on the next game, Evelyn? (*going to the table.*)

SIR J. Nonsense—nonsense—don't disturb him! All the fishes come to the bait! Sharks and minnows all nibbling away at my son-in-law. (*goes and takes the snuff-box.*)

EVE. One hundred pounds, Blount? Oh, yes! the finest gentleman is never too fine a gentleman to pick up a guinea. Done! Treble the stakes, Smooth!

SIR J. I'm on the rack! Be cool, Evelyn! take care, my dear boy! Be cool—be cool! (SMOOTH *shows his cards.*)

EVE. What—what? You have four queens!—five to the king. Confound the cards! a fresh pack. (*throws the cards behind him over* SIR JOHN. WAITER *brings a new pack of cards to* EVELYN.)

OLD MEM. Waiter! the snuff-box. (*murmurs. Different* MEMBERS *gather round.*)

Two MEMBERS *re-enter, and advance to* EVELYN's *table. All the* WAITERS *on.*

FLAT (*with back to audience*). I never before saw Evelyn out of temper. He must be losing immensely!

GREEN (R.). Yes—this is interesting!   .

SIR J. Interesting! There's a wretch!

FLAT (*next to* GREEN). Poor fellow! he'll be ruined in a month

SIR J. I'm in a cold sweat!

GREEN. Smooth is the very devil.

SIR J. The devil's a joke to him!

GLOSS. (*slapping* SIR JOHN *on the back*). A clever fellow that Smooth, Sir John, eh? (*takes up the snuff-box ;* OLD MEMBER *as before*) £100 on this game, Evelyn? (*going to the table.*)

EVE. (*half turning round*). You! well done the Constitution! yes, £100!

OLD MEM. Waiter! the snuff-box.

STOUT. I think I'LL venture £200 on this game, Evelyn? (*goes in front of table,* R.)

EVE. (*quite turning round*). Ha! ha! ha!—Enlightenment and the Constitution on the same side of the question at last! Oh, Stout, Stout! —greatest happiness of the greatest number—greatest number, number one! Done, Stout!—£200! ha! ha! deal, Smooth. Well done, Political Economy—ha! ha! ha!

SIR J. Quite hysterical—drivelling! Aren't you ashamed of yourselves? His own cousins—all in a conspiracy—a perfect gang of them. (*takes snuff-box as before.* MEMBERS *indignant.*)

STOUT (*to* MEMBERS). Hush! he's to marry Sir John's daughter!

FLAT. What! Stingy Jack's? oh!

CHORUS OF MEMS. Oh! oh!

EVE. By Heaven, there never was such luck! It's enough to drive a man wild! This is mere child's play, Smooth—double or quits on the whole amount!

SMOOTH. Anything to oblige! (*murmurs; they play quickly.*)

SIR J. Oh, dear—oh, dear! (*great excitement.*)

EVE. (*throwing down his cards, and rising in great agitation*). No more, no more—I've done!—quite enough! Glossmore, Stout, Blount—I'll pay you to-morrow. I—I—Death!—this is ruinous! (*crosses* L., *seizes the snuff-box, and goes up,* L. C., *to chair,* L. U. E.; *sits.*)

SIR J. *Ruinous?* What has he lost? what *has* he lost, Smooth? Not much? eh? eh? (MEMBERS *look at* EVELYN; *others gather round* SMOOTH, C.)

SMOOTH. Oh, a trifle, dear John!—excuse me! We never tell our winnings. (*to* BLOUNT, L.) How d'ye do, Fred?—(*to* GLOSSMORE, R.) By the bye, Charles, don't you want to sell your house in Grosvenor square? —£12,000, eh?

GLOSS. Yes, and the furniture at valuation. About £3,000 more.

SMOOTH (*looking over his pocket-book*). Um! Well, we'll talk of it.

SIR J. (L. C.). 12 and 3—£15,000. What a cold-blooded rascal it is! —£15,000, Smooth?

SMOOTH. Oh, the house itself is a trifle; but the establishment—I'm considering whether I have enough to keep it up, my dear John. (*goes* L.)

OLD MEM. Waiter! the snuff-box! (*scraping it round and with a wry face*) And it's all gone! (*gives it to the* WAITER *to fill.*)

SIR J. (*turning round*). And it's all gone!

EVE. (*starting up and laughing hysterically*). Ha! ha! all gone? not a bit of it. (*goes to* SMOOTH, C.) Smooth, this club is so noisy. Sir John, you are always in the way. Come to my house! come! Champagne and a broiled bone. Nothing venture, nothing have! The luck must turn, and by Jupiter we'll make a night of it! (*going;* SIR JOHN *stops him.*)

SIR J. A night of it! For Heaven's sake, Evelyn! EVELYN!—think what you are about!—think of Georgina's feelings!—think of your poor lost mother!—think of the babes unborn!—think of——

EVE. I'll think of nothing! Zounds!—you don't know what I have lost, man; it's all your fault, distracting my attention. Pshaw—pshaw! Out of the way, do! (*throws* SIR JOHN *off,* L.) Come, Smooth. Ha! ha! a night of it, my boy—a night of it! [*Exeunt* SMOOTH *and* EVELYN, C.

SIR J. (*following*). You must not—you shall not! Evelyn, my dear Evelyn! he's drunk—he's mad! Will no one send for the police! [*Exit,* C.

MEMS. Ha! ha! ha! Poor old Stingy Jack!

OLD MEM. (*rising for the first time, and in a great rage*). Waiter! the snuff-box!

MEMS. Ha! ha! ha! Stingy Jack! (*murmurs and laughter as the act-drop descends.*)

CURTAIN.

ACT IV.

SCENE I.—*An ante-room in* EVELYN'S *house.*

Enter TOKE, GLOSSMORE, *and* BLOUNT, R. *Chairs and tables with writing materials,* R. *and* L.

TOKE. My master is not very well, my lord; but I'll let him know.
[*Exit* TOKE, O. D.

GLOSS. I am very curious to learn the result of his gambling tete-à-tete. There are strange reports abroad, and the tradesmen have taken the alarm.

BLOUNT. Oh, he's so howwidly wich, he can afford even a tete-à-tete with Deadly Smooth!

GLOSS. Poor old Stingy Jack! why, Georgina was *your* intended.

BLOUNT. Yes; and I weally liked the girl, though out of pique I pwoposed to her cousin. But what can a man do against money?

Enter EVELYN, C., *in a morning wrapper.*

If we could start fair, you'd see whom Georgina would pwefer; but she's sacwificed by her father! She as much as told me so! (*crosses,* R.)

EVE. (*aside*). Now to work still further upon Sir John, through these excellent friends of mine. (*aloud*) So, so—good morning, gentlemen! we've a little account to settle—one hundred each.

BOTH. Don't talk of it.

EVE. (*putting up his pocket-book*). Well, I'll not talk of it. (*taking* BLOUNT *aside*) Ha! ha! you'd hardly believe it—but I'd rather not pay you just at present; my money is locked up, and I must wait, you know, for the Groginhole rents. So, instead of owing you £100, suppose I owe you *five?* You can give me a check for the other four. And, harkye! not a word to Glossmore.

BLOUNT. Glossmore! the gweatest gossip in London! I shall be delighted! (*aside*) It never does harm to lend to a wich man; one gets it back somehow. (*aloud*) By the way, Evelyn, if you want my gwey cabhorse, you may have him for £200, and that will make seven.

EVE. (*aside*). That's the fashionable usury; your friend does not take interest—he sells you a horse. (*aloud*) Blount, it's a bargain. (BLOUNT *goes to* R. *table.*)

BLOUNT (*writing a check, and musingly*). No; I don't see what harm it can do me; that off-leg must end in a spavin.

EVE. Now for my other friend. (*to* GLOSSMORE) That £100 I owe you is rather inconvenient at present; I've a large sum to make up for the Groginhole property—perhaps you would lend me five or six hundred more—just to go on with?

GLOSS. (L.). Certainly! Hopkins is dead;_your interest for Cipher wouid——

EVE. Why, I can't promise *that* at this moment. But as a slight mark of friendship and gratitude, I shall be very much flattered if you'll accept a splendid gray cab-horse I bought to-day—cost £200!

GLOSS. (*aside*). Bought *to-day*—then I'm safe. (*aloud*) My dear fellow, you're always so princely!

EVE. Nonsense! just write the check; and, harkye, not a syllable to Blount!

GLOSS. Blount! He's the town-crier! (*goes to write at* L. *table.*)

BLOUNT (*rises, giving* EVELYN *the check*). Wansom's, Pall-mall East.

EVE. Thank you. So you *proposed* to Miss Douglas!

BLOUNT (R.). Hang it! yes; I could have sworn that she fancied me; her manner, for instance, the vewy day you pwoposed for Miss Vesey, otherwise Georgina——

EVE. Has only half what Miss Douglas has.

BLOUNT. You forget how much Stingy Jack must have saved! But I beg your pardon.

EVE. Never mind; but not a word to Sir John, or he'll fancy I'm ruined. (GLOSSMORE *comes down,* L.)

GLOSS. (*giving the check*). Ransom's, Pall-mall East.   Tell me, did you win or lose last night ?

EVE. Win ! lose ! oh !   No more of that, if you love me.   I must send off at once to the banker's. (*looking at the two checks.*)

GLOSS. (*aside*). Why, he's borrowed from Blount, too !

BLOUNT (*aside*). That's a cheque from Lord Glossmore,

EVE. Excuse me ; I must dress ; I have not a moment to lose.   You remember you dine with me to-day—seven o'clock.   You'll meet Smooth. (*mournfully*) It may be the last time I shall ever welcome you here. My—what am I saying ?   Oh, merely a joke—good bye—*good* bye. (*shaking them heartily by the hand.   Exit, c. d.   GLOSSMORE and BLOUNT look at each other for a moment, and then speak.*)

BLOUNT. Glossmore !

GLOSS. Blount !

BLOUNT. I am afwaid all's not wight !

GLOSS. I incline to your opinion.

BLOUNT. But I've sold my gway cab-horse.

GLOSS. Gray cab-horse ! you !—What is he really worth now ?

BLOUNT. Since he is sold, I will tell you—Not a sixpence.

GLOSS. Not a sixpence ? he gave it to me.

BLOUNT. That was devilish unhandsome !   Do you know, I feel nervous !

GLOSS. Nervous !   Let us run and stop payment of our checks.

Enter TOKE, o. D. ; *he runs across the stage towards* R.

BLOUNT. Hollo, John ! where so fast ?

TOKE (*in great haste*). Beg pardon, Sir Frederick, to Pall-mall East—Messrs. Ransom.   . [*Exit*, R.

BLOUNT (*solemnly*) Glossmore, we are floored ?

GLOSS. Sir, the whole town shall know of it.   [*Exeunt*, R.

SCENE II.—*A splendid saloon in* EVELYN'S *house.   Doors* o., *leading to the dining-room.*

EVELYN *and* GRAVES *discovered seated.*

GRAVES. You don't mean to say you've borrowed money of Sir John ?

EVE. Yes, five hundred pounds.   Observe how I'll thank him for it ; observe how delighted he will be to find that five hundred was really of service to me.

GRAVES. I don't understand you.   You've grown so mysterious of late. You've withdrawn your money from Flash and Brisk ?

EVE. (R. *of* L. *table*). No.

GRAVES. No—then——

Enter SIR JOHN, LADY FRANKLIN, *and* GEORGINA, R.   GEORGINA *goes to table* L., *and listens to* EVELYN.   LADY FRANKLIN *and* GRAVES *up* C.

SIR J. You got the check for £500 safely—too happy to—(*grasping* EVELYN'S *hand.*)

EVE. (*interrupting him*). My best thanks—my warmest gratitude ! So kind in you ! so seasonable—that £500—you don't know the value of that £500.   I shall never forget your nobleness of conduct.

SIR J. Gratitude ! Nobleness ! (*aside*) I can't have been taken in ?

EVE. And in a moment of such distress !

SIR J. (*aside*). Such distress! He picks out the ugliest words in the whole dictionary.

EVE. You must know, my dear Sir John, I've done with Smooth. But I'm still a little crippled, and you must do me *another* favor. I've only as yet paid the deposit of ten per cent. for the great Groginhole property. I am to pay the rest this week—nay, I fear to-morrow. I've already sold out of the Funds for the purchase; the money lies at the bankers', and of course I can't touch it; for if I don't pay by a certain day, I forfeit the estate and the deposit.

SIR J. What's coming now, I wonder?

Enter SERVANT, R. *Announces* MR. STOUT *and exits. Enter* STOUT, *in evening dress.*

EVE. Georgina's fortune is £10,000. I always meant, my dear Sir John, to present you with that little sum.

SIR J. Oh, Evelyn! (*wipes his eyes;* STOUT *goes to* L. *table.*)

EVE. But the news of my losses has frightened my tradesmen! I have so many heavy debts at this moment that—that—that.—But I see Georgina is listening, and I'll say what I have to say to her. (*crosses to her,* R. C.)

SIR J. No, no—no, no. Girls don't understand business.

EVE. The very reason I speak to her. This is an affair not of business, but of *feeling.* Stout, show Sir John my Correggio.

SIR J. (*aside*). Devil take his Correggio! The man is born to torment me! (STOUT *takes him by the arm, and points off,* L. S. E.)

EVE. My dear Georgina, whatever you may hear said of me, I flatter myself that you feel confidence in my honor.

GEOR. Can you doubt it?

EVE. I confess that I am embarrassed at this moment; I have been weak enough to lose money at play. I promise you never to gamble again as long as I live. My affairs can be retrieved; but for the first few years of our marriage it may be necessary to retrench.

GEOR. Retrench!

EVE. To live, perhaps, altogether in the country.

GEOR. Altogether in the country!

EVE. To confine ourselves to a modest competence.

GEOR. Modest competence! I knew something horrid was coming.

Enter SIR F. BLOUNT, R.; *he salutes* EVELYN *and* LADY FRANKLIN.

EVE. And now, Georgina, you may have it in your power at this moment to save me from much anxiety and humiliation. My money is locked up—my debts of honor must be settled—you are of age—your £10,000 is in your own hands——

SIR J. (STOUT *listening as well as* SIR JOHN). I'm standing on hot iron.

EVE. If you could lend it to me for a few weeks. You hesitate. Can you give me this proof of your confidence? Remember, without confidence, what is wedlock?

SIR J. (*aside to her*). No! (EVELYN *turns sharply*) Yes, (*pointing his glass at the Correggio*) the painting may be fine.

STOUT. But you don't like the subject?

GEOR. (*aside*). He may be only trying me! Best leave it to papa.

EVE. Well——

GEOR. You—you shall hear from me to-morrow. (*aside*) Ah, there's that dear Sir Frederick! (*goes to* BLOUNT, *at the back.*)

Enter GLOSSMORE *and* SMOOTH, R.   EVELYN *salutes them, paying* SMOOTH *servile respect ; takes his arm and crosses to* L., *and up the stage.*

LADY F. (R. C., *to* GRAVES). Ha! ha! To be so disturbed yesterday—was it not droll?

GRAVES. Never recur to that humiliating topic.

GLOSS. (C., *to* STOUT). See how Evelyn fawns upon Smooth.

STOUT. How mean in him!—*Smooth*—a professional gambler—a fellow who lives by his wits. I would not know such a man on any account. (SMOOTH *comes down*, C.)

SMOOTH (*to* GLOSSMORE). So Hopkins is dead—you want Cipher to come in for Groginhole, eh?

GLOSS. (L. C.). What—could *you* manage it? (*aside*) Why, he must have won his whole fortune.

SMOOTH. *Ce cher, Charles!*—anything to oblige.

GLOSS. It is not possible he can have lost Groginhole!

STOUT. Groginhole!   What can he have done with Groginhole! Glossmore, present me to Smooth.

GLOSS. What! the gambler—the fellow who lives by his wits?

STOUT. Why, his wits seem to be an uncommonly productive capital? I'll introduce myself. (*crosses to* SMOOTH) How d'ye do, Captain Smooth? We have met at the club, I think—I am charmed to make your acquaintance in private.   I say, sir, what do you think of the affairs of the nation?   Bad! very bad—no enlightenment—great fall off in the revenue—no knowledge of finance!   There's only one man who can save the country—and that's Popkins!

SMOOTH. Is he in Parliament, Mr. Stout?   What's your Christian name, by-the-bye?

STOUT. Benjamin—No;—constituences are so ignorant they don't understand his value.   He's no orator; in fact, he stammers a little—that is, a great deal—but devilish profound.   Could not we ensure him for Groginhole?

SMOOTH. My dear Benjamin, it is a thing to be thought on. (*they retire.*)

EVE. (*advancing*). My friends, pray be seated. (*they sit**) I wish to consult you.   This day twelve months I succeeded to an immense income, and as, by a happy coincidence, on the same day I secured your esteem, so now I wish to ask you if you think I could have spent that income in a way more worthy your good opinion.

GLOSS. Impossible! excellent taste—beautiful house!

BLOUNT. Vewy good horses—(*aside, to* GLOSSMORE)—especially the gway cab.

LADY F. Splendid pictures!

GRAVES. And a magnificent cook, ma'am!

SMOOTH (*thrusting his hands into his pockets*). It is my opinion, Alfred—and I'm a judge—that you could not have spent your money better.

OMNES (*except* SIR JOHN). Very true!

GEOR. Certainly. (*coaxingly*) Don't retrench, my dear Alfred!

GLOSS. Retrench! nothing so plebeian!

STOUT. Plebeian, sir—worse than plebeian—it is against all rules of public morality.   Every one knows, now-a-days, that extravagance is a

---

* All sit thus.

SIR FREDERICK.	GLOSSMORE.	STOUT.	SMOOTH.	GEORGINA.
LADY FRANKLIN.				EVELYN.
GRAVES.				SIR JOHN.
R.				L.

benefit to the population—encourages art—employs labor—and multi-plies spinning-jennies.

Eve. You reassure me! I own I did think that a man worthy of friends so sincere might have done something better than feast—dress—drink—play——

Gloss. Nonsense—we like you the better for it. (*aside*) I wish I had my £600 back, though.

Eve. And you are as much my friends now as when you offered me £10 for my old nurse?

Sir J. A thousand times more so, my dear boy. (Omnes *approve.*)

Enter Sharp, r.

Smooth. But who's our new friend?

Eve. Who? the very man who first announced to me the wealth which you allow I have spent so well. But what's the matter, Sharp? (*crosses to* Sharp, *who whispers to him.*)

Eve. (*aloud*). The bank's *broke!* (*all start up.*)

Sir J. Bank broke—what bank? (*coming down*, c.)

Eve. Flash, Brisk and Co.

Sir J. But I warned you—you withdrew?

Eve. Alas! no!

Sir J. Oh! Not much in their hands?

Eve. Why, I told you the purchase-money for Groginhole was at my bankers'—but no, no; don't look so frightened! It was not placed with Flash—it is at Hoare's—it is, indeed. Nay, I assure you it is. A mere trifle at Flash's, upon my word, now! Don't groan in that way. You'll frighten everybody! To-morrow, Sharp, we'll talk of this! One day more—one day, at least for enjoyment. (*walks to and fro.*)

Sir J. Oh! a pretty enjoyment!
Blount. And he borrowed £700 of me!
Gloss. And £600 of me!
Sir J. And £500 of me!
Stout. Oh! a regular Jeremy Diddler!

All up the stage, l. *and*
l. c.

Stout (*to* Sir John). I say, you have placed your daughter in a very unsafe investment. Transfer the stock.

Sir J. (*going to* Georgina). Ha! I'm afraid we've been very rude to Sir Frederick. A monstrous fine young man!

Enter Toke, *with a letter*, r.

Toke (*to* Evelyn). Sir, I beg your pardon, but Mr. MacFinch insists on my giving you this letter instantly.

Eve. (*reading*). How! Sir John, this fellow, MacFinch, has heard of my misfortunes, and insists on being paid—a lawyer's letter—quite inso-lent. Here, read this letter—you'll be quite amused with it.

Toke. And, sir, Mr. Tabouret is below, and declares he will not stir till he's paid. [*Exit*, r.

Eve. Not stir till he's paid! What's to be done, Sir John? Smooth, what *is* to be done?

Smooth (*seated*, c.). If he'll not stir till he's paid, make him put up a bed, and I'll take him in the inventory, as one of the fixtures, Alfred.

Eve. It is very well for you to joke, Mr. Smooth. But——

Enter Sheriff's Officer, *giving a paper to* Evelyn *and whispering.*

Eve. What's this? Frantz, the tailor. Why, the impudent scoundrel ! Faith, this is more than I bargained for—Sir John, I'm arrested.

STOUT. He's arrested, (*slapping* SIR JOHN *on the back with glee*) old gentleman ! But I didn't lend him a farthing.

EVE. And for a mere song—£150 ! Sir John, pay this fellow, will you ? or see that my people kick out the bailiffs, or do it yourself, or something—while we go to dinner.

SIR J. Pay—kick—I'll be d—d if I do ! Oh, my £500 ! my £500 ! Mr. Alfred Evelyn, I want my £500 ! (GRAVES *and* LADY FRANKLIN *come forward.* R. C.)

GRAVES. I'm going to do a very silly thing—I shall lose both my friend and my money—just like my luck—Evelyn, go to dinner—I'll settle this for you.

LADY F. I love you for that !

GRAVES. Do you ? then I am the happiest—Ah ! ma'am, I don't know what I am saying ! (LADY FRANKLIN *retires*, R. *Exeunt* GRAVES *and* OF-FICER, R.)

EVE. (*to* GEORGINA, *who is* L. C.). Don't go by these appearances ! I repeat, £10,000 will more than cover all my embarrassments. I shall hear from you to-morrow ?

GEOR. Yes—yes ! (*going*, R.)

EVE. But you're not going ? You, too, Glossmore ? you, Blount ?—you, Stout ?—you, Smooth !

SMOOTH. No. I'll stick by you as long as you've a guinea to stake !

GLOSS. Oh, this might have been expected from a man of such am-biguous political opinions ! (*crosses*, R.)

STOUT. Don't stop me, sir. No man of common enlightenment would have squandered his substance in this way. Pictures and statues—baugh ! (*crosses*, R.)

EVE. Why, you all said I could not spend my money better ! Ha ! ha ! ha !—the absurdest mistake—you don't fancy I'm going to prison—Ha ! ha ! Why don't you laugh, Sir John ?—ha ! ha ! ha ! (*goes up the stage.* SIR JOHN *crosses to* R. C.)

SIR J. Sir, this horrible levity ! Take Sir Frederick's arm, my poor, injured, innocent child.

SMOOTH. But, my dear John, they have no right to arrest the dinner.

The C. *doors are thrown open by two* SERVANTS, *a handsome dining-room is discovered, and a table elegantly set for ten persons. Enter* TOKE, C.

TOKE. Dinner is served.

GLOSS. (*pausing*). Dinner !

STOUT. Dinner ! a very good smell !

EVE. (*to* SIR JOHN). Turtle and venison, too. (*they stop irresolute*) That's right—come along—come along—but one word first, Blount —Stout—Glossmore—Sir John—one word first ; will you lend me £10 for my old nurse ? (*they all fall back*) Ah, you fall back ! Be-hold a lesson for all who build friendship upon their fortune, and not their virtues. You lent me hundreds this morning to squander upon pleasure—you would refuse me £10 now to bestow upon benevolence. Go—we have done with each other—go.

[*Exeunt, indignantly*, R., *all but* EVELYN *and* SMOOTH.

Re-enter GRAVES, R.

GRAVES. Heyday ! what's all this ?

EVE. Ha ! ha !—the scheme prospers—the duper *is* duped ! Come, my friends—come ; when the standard of money goes down, in the great

battle between man and fate—why, a bumper to the brave hearts that
refuse to desert us.   [*Exeunt*, c. *door.*
    SMOOTH *and* GRAVES. Ha! ha! ha! (*ring down when* EVELYN *is seated.*)

                        CURTAIN.

                        ———

                        ACT V.

SCENE I.—* * * *'s *Club;* SMOOTH, GLOSSMORE—*four other* MEMBERS
                    *discovered.**

    GLOSS. Will his horses be sold, think you?
    SMOOTH. Very possibly, Charles—a fine stud—hum—ha! Waiter, a
glass of sherry! (SMOOTH *is at breakfast at the* L. *table, where the* OLD MEM-
BER *sat.*)
                Enter WAITER, c., *with sherry.*

    GLOSS. They say he must go abroad.
    SMOOTH. Well; 'tis the best time of year for travelling, Charles.
    GLOSS. We are all to be paid to-day; and that looks suspicious!
    SMOOTH. Very suspicious, Charles! Hum!—ah!
    GLOSS. (*rises and crosses to* SMOOTH). My dear fellow, you must know
the rights of the matter; I wish you'd speak out. What have you really
won? Is the house itself gone?
    SMOOTH. The house itself is certainly not gone, Charles, for I saw it
exactly in the same place this morning at half-past ten—it has not
moved an inch. (WAITER *gives a letter to* GLOSSMORE.)
    GLOSS. (*reading*). From Groginhole—an express! What's this? I'm
amazed! (*reading*) "They've actually, at the eleventh hour, started Mr.
Evelyn; and nobody knows what his politics are! We shall be beat!—
the Constitution is gone—CIPHER!" Oh! this is infamous in Evelyn!
Gets into Parliament just to keep himself out of the Bench!
    SMOOTH. He's capable of it.
    GLOSS. Not a doubt of it, sir! Not a doubt of it! The man saves
himself at the expense of his country—Groginhole is lost. There's an
end of the Constitution!   [*Exit,* c.

            Enter SIR JOHN *and* BLOUNT, c., *talking.*

    SIR J. My dear boy, I'm not flint! I am but a man! If Georgina
really loves you—and I am sure that she *does*—I will never think of sac-
rificing her happiness to ambition—she is yours; I told her so this very
morning.
    BLOUNT (*aside*). The old humbug!
    SIR J. She's the best of daughters! Dine with me at seven, and we'll
talk of the settlements. (WAITER *brings a bill on a salver to* SMOOTH; *he
pays it.*)
    BLOUNT. Yes; I don't care for fortune—but——
    SIR J. Her £10,000 will be settled on herself—that of course.
    BLOUNT. *All* of it, sir? Weally, I——
    SIR J. What *then*, my dear boy? I shall leave you both all I've laid
by. Ah, you know I'm a close fellow! "Stingy Jack,"—eh? After

——————————————————————————
        * This Scene is frequently omitted.

all, worth makes the man! (WAITER *removes breakfast things and cloth from* SMOOTH'S *table.*)

SMOOTH. (*rises*). And the more a man's worth, John, the worthier man he must be. (*Exeunt*, MEMBERS *and* SMOOTH, C. SIR JOHN *takes up a newspaper and reads.*)

BLOUNT (*aside*). Yes; he has no other child! She *must* have all his savings; I don't see what harm it could do me. Still, that £10,000—I want that £10,000; if she would but wun off one could get wid of the settlements.

Enter STOUT, C. (*wiping his forehead*), *and takes* SIR JOHN *aside*, L.

STOUT. Sir John, we've been played upon! My secretary is brother to Flash's head clerk; Evelyn had not £300 in the bank!

SIR J. (C.). Bless us and save us! you take away my breath! But then—Deadly Smooth—the execution—the—Oh, he must be done up!

STOUT. As to Smooth, he'd "do anything to oblige." All a trick, depend upon it. Smooth has already deceived me, for before the day's over, Evelyn will be member for Groginhole. I've had an express from Popkins; he's in despair! not for *himself*—but for the *country*, Sir John, —what's to become of the country?

SIR J. But what could be Evelyn's *object ?*

STOUT. *Object?* Do you look for an object in a whimsical creature like that?—a man who has not even any political opinions! Object! Perhaps to break off his match with your daughter! Take care, Sir John, or the borough will be lost to your family.

SIR J. Aha! I begin to smell a rat.

STOUT. Do you?

SIR J. But it is not too late yet.

STOUT. My interest in Popkins made me run to Lord Spendquick, the late proprietor of Groginhole. I told him that Evelyn could not pay the rest of the money! and *he* told me that——

SIR J. What?

STOUT. Mr. Sharp had just paid it him; there's no hope for Popkins! England will rue this day. (*goes to table and looks at papers.*)

SIR J. *Georgina* shall lend him the money! *I'll* lend him—every man in my house shall lend him—I feel again what it is to be a father-in-law—Sir Frederick, excuse me—you can't dine with me to-day. And, on second thoughts, I see that it would be very unhandsome to desert poor Evelyn, now he's down in the world. Can't think of it, my dear boy—can't think of it! Very much honored, and happy to see you as a friend. Waiter, my carriage! Um! What, humbug *Stingy Jack*, will they? Ah! a good joke, indeed.   [*Exit*, c.

BLOUNT. Mr. Stout, what have you been saying to Sir John? Something about my chawacter; I know you have; don't deny it. Sir, I shall expect satisfaction!

STOUT. Satisfaction, Sir Frederick? Pooh, as if a man of enlightenment had any satisfaction in fighting! Did not mention your name; we were talking of Evelyn. Only think—he's no more ruined than you are.

BLOUNT. Not wuined! Aha, now I understand! So, so! Stay, let me see—she's to meet me in the square. (*pulls out his watch; a very small one.*)

STOUT (*pulling out his own; a very large one*). I must be off to the vestry.   [*Exit*, C.

BLOUNT. Just in time—ten thousand pounds! 'Gad, my blood's up, and I won't be tweated in *this* way if he were fifty times Stingy Jack!
                                                                   [*Exit*, c.

SCENE II.—*The drawing-rooms in* SIR JOHN VESEY'S *house.*

Enter LADY FRANKLIN *and* GRAVES, L.

GRAVES. Well, well, I am certain that poor Evelyn loves Clara still, but you can't persuade me that she cares for him.

LADY F. She has been breaking her heart ever since she heard of his distress. Nay, I am sure she would give all she has, could it save him from the consequences of his own folly.

GRAVES. I should just like to sound her.

LADY F. (*ringing the bell*). And you shall. I take so much interest in her, that I forgive your friend everything but his offer to Georgina.

Enter PAGE, R.

Where are the young ladies?

PAGE. Miss Vesey is, I believe, still in the square; Miss Douglas is just come in, my lady.

LADY F. What! did she go out with Miss Vesey?

PAGE. No, my lady; I attended her to Drummond's, the banker.

[*Exit*, R.

LADY F. Drummond's!

Enter CLARA. R.

Why, child, (*crosses to her*) what on earth could take you to Drummond's at this hour of the day?

CLARA (*confused*). Oh, I—that is—I—Ah, Mr. Graves! (*crosses to* GRAVES) How is Mr. Evelyn? How does he bear up against so sudden a reverse?

GRAVES. With an awful calm. I fear all is not right here! (*touching his head*) The report in the town is, that he must go abroad instantly—perhaps to-day. (*crosses to* C.)

CLARA (C.). Abroad!—to-day!

GRAVES (L.). But all his creditors will be paid; and he only seems anxious to know if Miss Vesey remains true in his misfortunes.

CLARA. Ah! he loves her so *much*, then?

GRAVES. Um! That's more than I can say.

CLARA. She told me last night, that he said £10,000 would free him from all his liabilities—that was the sum, was it not?

GRAVES. Yes; he persists in the same assertion. Will Miss Vesey lend it?

LADY F. (*aside*, R.). If she does, I shall not think so well of her poor dear mother; for I am sure she'd be no child of Sir John's!

GRAVES. I should like to convince myself that my poor friend has nothing to hope from a woman's generosity.

LADY F. Civil! And are men, then, less covetous?

GRAVES. I know one man at least, who, rejected in his poverty by one as poor as himself, no sooner came into a sudden fortune than he made his lawyer invent a codicil which the testator never dreamt of, bequeathing independence to the woman who had scorned him.

LADY F. And never told her?

GRAVES. Never! There's no such document at Doctors' Commons, depend on it. You seem incredulous, Miss Clara! Good day! (*crosses*, R.)

CLARA (*following him*). One word, for mercy's sake! Do I understand you right? Ah, how could I be so blind? Generous Evelyn!

GRAVES. *You* appreciate, and *Georgina* will desert him. Miss Douglas, he loves you still. If that's not just like me! Meddling with other people's affairs, as if they were worth it—hang them! [*Exit*, R.

CLARA. Georgina will desert him. Do you think so?

LADY F. She told me last night that she would never see him again. To do her justice, she's less interested than her father—and as much attached as she can be to another. Even while engaged to Evelyn, she has met Sir Frederick every day in the square.

CLARA. And he is alone—sad—forsaken—ruined. And I, whom he enriched—I, the creature of his bounty—I, once the woman of his love —I stand idly here to content myself with tears and prayers! Oh, Lady Franklin, have pity on me—on him! We are both of kin to him—as relations we have both a right to comfort! Let us go to him—come!

LADY F. No! it would scarcely be right—remember the world—I cannot!

CLARA. All abandon him—then I will go alone! (*crosses*, R.)

LADY F. Alone—what will he think? What but——

CLARA. What but—that, if he love me still, I may have enough for both, and I am by his side! But that is too bright a dream. He told me I might call him brother! Where, now, should a sister be? But— but—I—I—I—tremble! If, after all—if—if—In one word, am I too bold? The world—my conscience can answer *that*—but do you think that *he* could despise me?

LADY F. No, Clara, no! Your fair soul is too transparent for even libertines to misconstrue. Something tells me that this meeting may make the happiness of both. You cannot go alone. My presence justifies all. Give me your hand—we will go together. [*Exeunt*, R.

SCENE III.—*A room in* EVELYN'S *house, same as last of Act IV*. EVELYN *discovered at table*, R.

EVE. Yes; as yet, all surpasses my expectations. I am sure of Smooth—I have managed even Sharp; my election will seem but an escape from a prison. Ha! ha! True, it cannot last long; but a few hours more are all I require, and for that time at least I shall hope to be thoroughly ruined. (*rises and goes* L.)

Enter GRAVES, R.

Well, Graves, and what do people say of me?

GRAVES. Everything that's bad!

EVE. Three days ago I was universally respected. I awake this morning to find myself singularly infamous. Yet, I'm the same man.

GRAVES. Humph! why, gambling——

EVE. Cant! it was not criminal to gamble—it was criminal to lose. Tut!—will you deny that if I had ruined Smooth instead of myself, every hand would have grasped mine yet more cordially, and every lip would have smiled congratulation on my success? Man—Man—I've not been rich and poor for nothing. The Vices and the Virtues are written in a language the world cannot construe; it reads them in a vile translation, and the translators are—*failure* and *success!* You alone are unchanged.

GRAVES. There's no merit in that I am always ready to mingle my tears with any man. (*aside*) I know I'm a fool, but I can't help it. (*aloud*) Hark ye, Evelyn, I like you—I'm rich; and anything I can do to get you out of your hobble will give me an excuse to grumble for the rest of my life. There, now 'tis out.

EVE. (*touched*). There's something good in human nature, after all!

My dear friend, I will now confide in you; I am not the spendthrift you think me—my losses have been trifling—not a month's income of my fortune. (GRAVES *shakes him heartily by the hand*) No! it has been but a stratagem to prove if the love, on which was to rest the happiness of a whole life, were given to the Money or the Man. Now you guess why I have asked from Georgina this one proof of confidence and affection.— Think you she will give it?

GRAVES. Would you break your heart if she did not?

EVE. It is vain to deny that I still love Clara; our last conversation renewed feelings which would task all the energies of my soul to conquer. No! the heart was given to the soul as its ally, not as its traitor.

GRAVES. What do you intend to do?

EVE. This:—If Georgina prove, by her confidence and generosity, that she loves me for myself, I will shut Clara for ever from my thoughts. I am pledged to Georgina, and I will carry to the altar a soul resolute to deserve her affection and fulfill its vows.

GRAVES. And if she reject you?

EVE. (*joyfully*). If she do, I am free once more! And then—then I will dare to ask, for I can ask without dishonor, if Clara can explain the past and bless the future! (*crosses*, R.)

Enter SERVANT, R., *with a letter on a salver ;* EVELYN *takes it.   Exit* SER-
VANT, R.

EVE. (*after reading it*). The die is cast—the dream is over. Generous girl! Oh, Georgina! I will deserve you yet.

GRAVES. Georgina! is it possible?

EVE. And the delicacy, the womanhood, the exquisite grace of this! How we misjudge the depth of the human heart! How, seeing the straws on the surface, we forget that the pearls may lie hid below! I imagined her incapable of this devotion.

GRAVES. And *I, too.*

EVE. It were base in me to continue this trial a moment longer; I will write at once to undeceive that generous heart. (*goes to* R. *table and writes.*)

GRAVES. I would have given £1,000 if that little jade Clara had been beforehand. But just like my luck; if I want a man to marry one woman, he's sure to marry another on purpose to vex me.

EVE. Graves, will you ring the bell? (GRAVES *rings bell*, L.)

Enter SERVANT, R.

Take this instantly to Miss Vesey ; say I will call in an hour. (*exit* SER-VANT.) And now Clara is resigned forever. Why does my heart sink within me? Why, why, looking to the fate to come, do I see only the memory of what has been? (*goes towards* L.)

GRAVES. You are re-engaged then to Georgina?

EVE. Irrevocably.

Enter SERVANT, R., *announcing* LADY FRANKLIN *and* MISS DOUGLAS.

LADY F. My dear Evelyn, you may think it strange to receive such visitors at this moment; but, indeed, it is no time for ceremony. We are your relations—it is reported you are about to leave the country— we come to ask frankly what we can do to serve you!

EVE. Madam—I——

LADY F. Come, come—do not hesitate to confide in us; Clara is less

a stranger to you than I am; your friend here will perhaps let me consult with him. (*crosses and speaks aside to* GRAVES) Let us leave them to
themselves.

GRAVES. You're an angel of a widow; but you come too late, as whatever is good for anything generally does. (*they retire into the inner-room,
out of sight, the doors of which should be partially open.*)

EVE. (L.). Miss Douglas, I may well want words to thank you! this
goodness—this sympathy——

CLARA (R., *abandoning herself to her emotion*). Evelyn! Evelyn! Do
not talk thus! Goodness! sympathy—I have learned *all—all!* It is
for ME to speak of *gratitude!* What! even when I had so wounded you
—when you believed me mercenary and cold—when you thought that I
was blind and base enough not to know you for what you are; even *at
that time* you thought but of my happiness—my fortunes—my fate!—
And to you—you—I owe all that has raised the poor orphan from servi-
tude and dependence! While your words were so bitter, your deeds so
gentle! Oh, noble Evelyn, this then was your revenge.

EVE. You owe me no thanks—that revenge was sweet! Think you it
was nothing to feel that my presence haunted you, though you knew it
not?—that in things the pettiest as the greatest, which that gold could
buy—the very jewels you wore—the very robe in which, to other eyes,
you might seem more fair—in all in which you took the woman's young
and innocent delight—*I* had a part—a share! that, even if separated
for ever—even if another's—even in distant years—perhaps in a happy
home, listening to sweet voices that might call you "mother!"—even
then should the uses of that dross bring to your lips one smile—that
smile was mine—due to me—due as a sacred debt, to the hand that you
rejected—to the love that you despised!

CLARA. Despised! See the proof that I despise you—see; in this
hour, when they say you are again as poor as before, I forget the world
—my pride—perhaps too much my sex; I remember but your sorrows
—I am here!

EVE. And is this the same voice that, when I knelt at your feet—when
I asked but *one day* the hope to call you mine—spoke only of poverty,
and answered, "*Never?*"

CLARA. Because I had been unworthy of your love if I had insured
your misery! Evelyn, hear me! My father, like you, was poor—generous; gifted, like you, with genius—ambition; sensitive, like you, to
the least breath of insult. He married, as you would have done—married one whose only dower was penury and care! Alfred, I saw that
genius the curse to itself—I saw that ambition wither to despair—I saw
the struggle—the humiliation—the proud man's agony—the bitter life—
the early death—and heard over his breathless clay my mother's groan
of self-reproach! Alfred Evelyn, now speak! Was the woman you
loved so nobly to repay you with such a doom?

EVE. Clara, we should have shared it.

CLARA. Shared? Never let the woman who really loves comfort her
selfishness with such delusion! In marriages like this, the wife cannot
share the burden; it is he—the husband—to provide, to scheme, to work,
to endure—to grind out his strong heart at the miserable wheel! The
wife, alas! cannot share the struggle—she can but witness the despair!
And therefore, Alfred. I rejected you.

EVE. Yet you believe me as poor now as I was then?

CLARA. But *I* am not poor; *we* are not so poor. Of this fortune,
which is all your own—if, as I hear, one-half would free you from your
debts, why, we have the other half still left. Evelyn, it is humble—but
it is not penury. You know me now.

EVE. Know you! Bright angel, too excellent for man's harder nature to understand—at least it is permitted me to revere. Why were such blessed words not vouchsafed to me before?—why, why come they now —too late? Oh, Heaven—too late!

CLARA. Too late! What, then, have I said?

EVE. Wealth! what is it without you? *With* you, I recognize its power; to forestall your every wish—to smooth your every path—to make all that life borrows from Grace and Beauty your ministrant and handmaid;—why, *that* were to make gold indeed a god! But vain— vain—vain! Bound by every tie of faith, gratitude, loyalty, and honor, to another!

CLARA. Another! Is she, then, true to your reverses? I did not know this—indeed I did not! And I have thus betrayed myself! (*aside*) O, shame! he must despise me now! (CLARA *goes up and sits at table, R.*)

Enter SIR JOHN, R.; *at the same time* GRAVES *and* LADY FRANKLIN *advance from the inner room.*

SIR J. (*with dignity and frankness*). Evelyn, I was hasty yesterday. You must own it natural that I should be so. But Georgina has been so urgent in your defence—(*as* LADY FRANKLIN *comes down,* R.) Sister, just shut the door, will you?—that I cannot resist her. What's money without happiness? So give me your security; for she insists on lending you the £10,000.

EVE. I know, and have already received it.

SIR J. (C.—*aside*). Already received it! Is he joking? Faith, for the last two days I believe I have been living amongst the Mysteries of Udolpho! (*aloud*) Sister, have you seen Georgina?

LADY F. (R.). Not since she went out to walk in the square.

SIR J. (*aside*). She's not in the square, nor the house—where the deuce can the girl be?

EVE. I have written to Miss Vesey—I have asked her to fix the day for our wedding.

SIR J. (*joyfully*). Have you? Go, Lady Franklin, find her instantly —she must be back by this time; take my carriage—it is but a step— you will not be two minutes gone. (*aside*) I'd go myself, but I'm afraid of leaving him a moment while he's in such excellent dispositions.

LADY F. (*repulsing* CLARA, *who rises to follow*). No, no; stay till I return.   [*Exit, R.*

SIR J. And don't be down-hearted, my dear fellow; if the worst come to the worst, you will have everything I can leave you. Meantime, if I can in any way help you——

EVE. Ha!—you!—*you*, too? Sir John, you have seen my letter to Miss Vesey?—(*aside*) or could she have learned the truth before she ventured to be generous?

SIR J. No! on my honor. I only just called at the door on my way from Lord Spend—that is, from the City. Georgina was out;—was ever anything so unlucky? (*Voices without*—" Hurrah—hurrah! Blue for ever!") What's that?

Enter SHARP, R.

SHARP. Sir, a deputation from Groginhole—poll closed in an hour— you are returned! Holloa, sir—holloa!

EVE. (*aside*). And it was to please Clara!

SIR J. Mr. Sharp—Mr. Sharp—I say, how much has Mr. Evelyn lost by Messrs. Flash and Co.?

SHARP. Oh, a great deal, sir—a great deal!

Sir J. (*alarmed*). How?—a great deal!

Eve. Speak the truth, Sharp—concealment is all over. (*goes up the stage.*)

Sharp. £223 6s. 3d.—a great sum to throw away!

Sir J. Eh! what, my dear boy?—what? Ha! ha! all humbug, was it?—all humbug! So, Mr. Sharp, isn't he ruined, after all?—not the least wee, rascally little bit in the world ruined?

Sharp. Sir, he has never even lived up to his income.

Sir J. Worthy man! I could jump to the ceiling! I am the happiest father-in-law in the three kingdoms. (*knocking*, R.) And that's my sister's knock, too!

Clara (*rises*, R.). Since I was mistaken, cousin—since now you do not need me—forget what has passed; my business here is over. Farewell!

Eve. Could you but see my heart at this moment, with what love, what veneration, what anguish it is filled, you would know how little, in the great calamities of life, fortune is really worth. And must we part now, —*now*, when—when—I——

Enter Lady Franklin *and* Georgina, R., *followed by* Blount, *who looks shy and embarrassed;* Clara *retires and goes to* L. *table.*

Graves. Georgina herself—then there's no hope.

Sir J. (L.—*aside*). What the deuce brings that fellow Blount here? (*aloud*) Georgy, my dear Georgy, I want to——

Eve. (C.). Stand back, Sir John!

Sir J. But I must speak a word to her—I want to——

Eve. Stand back, I say—not a whisper—not a sign. If your daughter is to be my wife, to *her* heart only will I look for a reply to *mine.*— Georgina, it is true, then, that you trust me with your confidence—your fortune? It is also true, that when you did so you believed me ruined? Oh, pardon the doubt! Answer as if your father stood not there—answer me from that truth the world cannot yet have plucked from your soul—answer me as woman's heart, yet virgin and unpolluted, *should* answer to one who has trusted to it his all!

Geor. (R. C.—*aside*). What can he mean?

Sir J. (L. C.—*making signs*). She'll not look this way—she will not— hang her—Hem!

Eve. You falter. I implore—I adjure you—answer!

Lady F. Speak! (Sir John *makes an effort to speak ;* Evelyn *observes it.*)

Eve. Silence, Sir John!

Geor. Mr. Evelyn, your fortune might well dazzle me, as it dazzled others. Believe me, I sincerely pity your reverses.

Sir J. Good girl!—you hear her, Evelyn.

Geor. What's money without happiness?

Sir J. Clever creature!—my own sentiments!

Geor. And so, as our engagement is now annulled——

Eve. Annulled!

Geor. Papa told me so this very morning—I have promised my hand where I have given my heart—to Sir Frederick Blount. (Clara *goes down*, L.)

Sir J. I told you—I—No such thing—no such thing; you frighten her out of her wits—she don't know what's she's saying! (*goes up and over to* R.)

Eve. Am I awake? But this letter—this letter, received to-day——

Lady F. (*looking over the letter*). Drummond's—from a banker!

Eve. Read—read!

LADY F. "£10,000 just placed to your account—from the same unknown friend to Evelyn." Oh, Clara, I know now why you went to Drummond's this morning.

EVE. Clara! What!—and the former note with the same signature, on the faith of which I pledged my hand and sacrificed my heart——

LADY F. Was written under my eyes, and the secret kept that——

EVE. I see it all—how could I be so blind? I am free!—I am released!—Clara, you forgive me?—you love me?—you are mine! We are rich—rich! I can give you fortune, power—I can devote to you my whole life, thought, heart, soul—I am all yours, Clara—my own—my wife! (*kneels; she gives him her hand; they embrace.*)

SIR J. (*to* GEORGINA). A pretty mess you've made, to humbug your own father! And you too, Lady Franklin—I am to thank you for this! (EVELYN *places* CLARA *in a chair up* L.)

LADY F. You've to thank me that she's not now on the road to Scotland with Sir Frederick. I chanced on them by the Park just in time to dissuade and save her. But, to do her justice, a hint of your displeasure was sufficient.

GEOR. (*half-sobbing*). And you know, papa, you said this very morning that poor Frederick had been very ill-used, and you would settle it all at the club.

BLOUNT. Come, Sir John, you can only blame yourself and Evelyn's cunning device. After all, I'm no such vewy bad match; and as for the £10,000——

EVE I'll double it. Ah, Sir John, what's money without happiness? (*slaps* SIR JOHN *on the shoulder and retires.*)

SIR J. Pshaw—nonsense—stuff! Don't humbug me!

LADY F. But if you don't consent, she'll have no husband at all.

SIR J. Hum! there's something in that. (*aside to* EVELYN) Double it, will you? Then, settle it all *tightly* on her. Well—well—my foible is not avarice. Blount, make her happy. Child, I forgive you. (*pinching her arm*) Ugh, you fool! (BLOUNT *and* GEORGINA *go up,* L.)

GRAVES (*comes forward with* LADY FRANKLIN). I'm afraid it's catching. What say you? I feel the symptoms of matrimony creeping all over me. Shall we, eh? Frankly, now, frankly——

LADY F. Frankly, now, there's my hand.

GRAVES. Accepted. Is it possible? Sainted Maria! thank Heaven you are spared this affliction! (*goes up* C.)

Enter SMOOTH, R.

SMOOTH. How d'ye do, Alfred? I intrude, I fear! Quite a family party.

BLOUNT. Wish us joy, Smooth—Georgina's mine, and——

SMOOTH. And our four friends there apparently have made up another rubber. John, my dear boy, yon look as if you had something a, stake on the odd trick. (*crosses to* L.)

SIR J. Sir, your very—Confound the fellow—and he's a dead shot, too!

Enter STOUT *and* GLOSSMORE *hastily, talking with each other,* R.

GLOSS. My dear Evelyn, you were out of humor yesterday—but I forgive you. (EVELYN *takes his hand.*)

STOUT. Certainly! (EVELYN *crosses,* C.) what would become of public life if a man were obliged to be two days running in the same mind?—I rise to explain. Just heard of your return, Evelyn. Congratulate you.

The great motion of the session is fixed for Friday. We count on your vote. Progress with the times.

GLOSS. Preserve the Constitution!

STOUT. Your money will do wonders for the party! Advance!

GLOSS. The party respects men of your property. Stick fast!

EVE. I have the greatest respect, I assure you, for the worthy and intelligent flies upon both sides of the wheel; but whether we go too fast or too slow does not, I fancy, depend so much on the flies as on the Stout Gentleman who sits inside and pays the post-boys. Now, all my politics as yet is to consider what's best for the Stout Gentleman!

SMOOTH. Meaning John Bull. *Ce cher*, old John! (EVELYN *crosses to* SMOOTH *and takes his hand.*)

EVE. Smooth, we have yet to settle our first piquet account and our last. And I sincerely thank you for the service you have rendered to me, and the lesson you have given these gentlemen. (*returns to* C.; *all the characters take their positions for the end. Turning to* CLARA) Ah, Clara, you—you have succeeded where wealth had failed! You have reconciled me to the world and to mankind. My friends—we must confess it—amidst the humors and the follies, the vanities, deceits, and vices that play their parts in the great Comedy of Life—it is our own fault if we do not find such natures, though rare and few, as redeem the rest, brightening the shadows that are flung from the form and body of the *time* with glimpses of the everlasting holiness of truth and love.

GRAVES. But for the truth and the love, when found, to make us tolerably happy, we should not be without——

LADY F. Good health;

GRAVES. Good spirits;

CLARA. A good heart;

SMOOTH. An innocent rubber;

GEOR. Congenial tempers;

BLOUNT. A pwoper degwee of pwudence;

STOUT. Enlightened opinions;

GLOSS. Constitutional principles;

SIR J. Knowledge of the world;

EVE. And—plenty of money!

Disposition of the Characters at the fall of the Curtain.

	CLARA.	EVELYN.	
BLOUNT.			LADY FRANKLIN.
GEORGINA.			GRAVES.
GLOSSMORE.			SMOOTH.
STOUT.			SIR JOHN.
R.			L.

CURTAIN.

☞ *Please notice that nearly all the Comedies, Farces and Comediettas in the following List of "DE WITT'S ACTING PLAYS" are very suitable for representation in small Amateur Theatres and on Parlor Stages, as they need but little extrinsic aid from complicated scenery or expensive costumes. They have attained their deserved popularity by their droll situations, excellent plots, great humor and brilliant dialogues, no less than by the fact that they are the most perfect in every respect of any edition of Plays ever published either in the United States or Europe, whether as regards purity of the text, accuracy and fulness of stage directions and scenery, or elegance of typography and clearness of printing.*

*** In ordering, please copy the figures at the commencement of each piece, which indicate the number of the piece in "DE WITT'S LIST OF ACTING PLAYS."

☞ Any of the following Plays sent, postage free, on receipt of price—fifteen cents.

Address,   ROBERT M. DE WITT,
No. 33 Rose Street, New York.

DE WITT'S ACTING PLAYS.

No.

1 CASTE. An original Comedy in three acts, by T. W. Robertson. A lively and effective satire upon the times, played successfully in America, at Wallack's. Five male and three female characters. Costumes, modern. Scenery, the first and third acts, interior of a neat room ; the second a fashionable room. Time in representation, two hours and forty minutes.

2 NOBODY'S CHILD. A romantic Drama in three acts, by Watts Phillips. Eighteen male and three female characters. A domestic drama, wonderfully successful in London, as it abounds in stirring scenes and capital situations. Costumes modern, suited to rural life in Wales. Scenery is wild and picturesque. Time in represeutation, two hours and a quarter.

3 £100,000. An original Comedy in three acts, by Henry J. Byron. Eight male and four female characters. A most effective piece, played with applause at Wallack's. Costumes of the day. Two scenes are required—a comfortably furnished parlor and an elegant apartment. Time in representation, one hour and three quarters.

DE WITT'S ACTING PLAYS.

No.

53 GERTRUDE'S MONEY BOX. A Farce in one act, by Harry Lemon. Four male and two female characters. A successful, well written piece; an incident in rural life. Costumes of the present time. Scene, interior of a cottage. Time in representation, forty-five minutes.

54 THE YOUNG COLLEGIAN (The Cantab). A Farce in one act, by T. W. Robertson. Three male and two female characters. A rattling piece, filled with ludicrous situations, which could be splendidly worked up by a good light comedian. Costumes modern; and scene, a handsome interior. Time in representation, fifty minutes.

55 CATHARINE HOWARD; or, the Throne, the Tomb and the Scaffold. An historical play in three acts [from the celebrated play of that name, by Alexander Dumas]; adapted by W: D. Suter. Twelve male and five female characters. A most successful acting drama in both France and England. Costumes of the period of Henry VIII of England, artistic and rich. Scenery elaborate and historical. Time in representation, two hours and a half.

56 TWO GAY DECEIVERS; or, Black, White and Gray. A Farce in one act by T. W. Robertson. Three male characters. Adapted from the French of one of the most laughable vaudevilles on the Parisian stage. Costumes of present day. Scene, a cell in a police station. Time in representation, forty minutes.

57 NOEMIE. A Drama in two acts, translated and adapt- ed from the French of Dennery and Clement by T. W. Robertson. Four male and four female characters. Originally acted in Paris, this piece created such a sensation that it was produced subsequently at all the leading theatres of London. Costumes modern. Scenery, a garden scene and a richly furnished interior. Time in representation, one hour and a half. Easily put on the stage.

58 DEBORAH (LEAH); or, the Jewish Maiden's Wrong. A Drama in three acts, by Charles Smith Cheltnam. Seven male and six female characters. A strangely effective acting play. Costumes picturesque yet simple. Scenery elaborate and cumbersome to handle. Time in representation, two hours and fifteen minutes. Elegant extracts can be taken from this drama.

59 THE POST BOY. An original Drama in two acts, by H. T. Craven. Five male and three female characters. Very successful. Costumes modern. Scenery, two interiors. Time of playing, an hour and a half.

60 THE HIDDEN HAND; or, the Gray Lady of Perth Vennon. A Drama in four acts, by Tom Taylor. Five male and five female characters. Costumes of the period of James II of England. Scenery somewhat elaborate. Time in representation, two hours and a half.

61 PLOT AND PASSION. A Drama in three acts [from the French], by Tom Taylor. Seven male and two female characters. A neat and well constructed play, admirably adapted to amateur representation. Costumes of the period of the First Empire, rich and attractive. Scenes, an interior in a French mansion, and one in a country villa. Time in representation, one hour and a half.

62 A PHOTOGRAPHIC FIX. A Farce in one act, by Frederick Hay. Three male and two female characters. A brilliant, witty production. Costumes of the day. Scene, a photographic room. Time in representation, thirty-five minutes.

63 MARRIAGE AT ANY PRICE. A Farce in one act, by J. P. Wooler. Five male and three female characters. A decided success in London. Costumes of the day. Two scenes, a plain chamber and a garden. Time in representation, thirty minutes.

64 A HOUSEHOLD FAIRY. A domestic Sketch in one act, by Francis Talfourd. One male and one female character. A gem in its line; artistic, dramatic and very natural. Modern costumes, and scene a poorly furnished apartment. Time in playing, twenty-five minutes.

77 THE ROLL OF THE DRUM. A romantic Drama in three acts, by Thomas Egerton Wilks. Eight male and four female characters. A standard piece with the British theatres. Costumes of the period of the first French revolution. Scenery, interior of a farm house, a picturesque landscape and a drawing room. Time in representation, one hour and forty-five minutes.

78 SPECIAL PERFORMANCES. A Farce in one act, by Wilmot Harrison. Seven male and three female characters. A most ludicrous, ingenious and sprightly production. Dresses of the present day. Scene, a chamber. Time in performance, forty minutes.

79 A SHEEP IN WOLF'S CLOTHING. A domestic Drama in one act, freely adapted from Madame de Girardin's "*Une Femme qui deteste Son Mari*," by Tom Taylor. Seven male and five female characters. A neat and pleasing domestic play, founded upon incidents following Monmouth's rebellion. Costumes of the time of James II of England. Scene, a tapestried chamber. Time of playing, one hour.

80 A CHARMING PAIR. A Farce in one act, by Thomas J. Williams. Four male and three female characters. Costumes of the present day. Scene, a handsomely furnished apartment. Time in representation, forty minutes.

81 VANDYKE BROWN. A Farce in one act, by Adolphus Charles Troughton. Three male and three female characters. Popular wherever performed. Costumes of the present day. Scene, a chamber, backed by a window. Time of representation, one hour.

82 PEEP O' DAY; or, Savourneen Dheelish. An Irish romantic Drama in four acts (derived from "Tales of the O'Hara Family"), by Edmund Falconer. The New "Drury Lane" version. Twelve male and four female characters. Costumes, Irish, in the year 1798. Scenery, illustrative of Munster. Time in representation, three hours.

83 THRICE MARRIED. A personation piece in one act, by Howard Paul. Six male and one female characters. The lady sings, dances and assumes personification of a French vocalist, of a Spanish dancer and of a man of fashion. Costumes of the day. Scene, a room in a lodging house. Time in representation, three quarters of an hour.

84)T GUILTY. A Drama in four acts, by Watts Phillips, en male and six female characters. A thrilling drama found upon a fact. Costumes of the present day. Scenery illustrative of localities about Southampton and its harbor, and of others in India. Time in representation, three hours.

85 LOCKED IN WITH A LADY. A Sketch from Life, by H. R. Addison. One male and one female character. A very pleasing and humorous interlude. Costume of the day, and scene a bachelor's apartment. Time in representation, thirty-five minutes.

86 THE LADY OF LYONS; or, Love and Pride. A Play in five acts, by Lord Lytton (Sir Edward Lytton Bulwer). Twelve male five female characters. Four of the male characters are very good ones; and Pauline, Madame Deschapelles and the Widow Melnotte are each excellent in their line. The piece abounds in eloquent declamation and sparkling dialogue. This edition is the most complete in all respects ever issued. It occupies three hours in representation. The scenery, gardens and interior of cottage and mansion. Costumes French, of 1795.

87 LOCKED OUT. A Comic Scene, illustrative of what may occur after dark in a great metropolis; by Howard Paul. One male and two female characters, with others unimportant. Scene, a street; dress, modern. Time in playing, thirty minutes.

88 FOUNDED ON FACTS. A Farce in one act, by J. P. Wooler. Four male and two female characters. A favorite acting piece, easily put on the stage and never failing in success. Costumes of the present day. Scene, a hotel parlor. Time in representation, thirty-five minutes.

No.

89 AUNT CHARLOTTE'S MAID. A Farce in one act, by J. Maddison Morton. Three male and three female characters. One of the best of this prolific humorist's dramatic pieces. Dresses of the period, and scene an apartment in a dwelling house. Time in representation, forty minutes.

90 ONLY A HALFPENNY. A Farce in one act, by John Oxenford. Two male and two female characters. Dresses of the present day, and scene an elegantly furnished interior. Time in representation, thirty-five minutes.

91 WALPOLE; or, Every Man has his Price. A Comedy in rhyme, by Lord Lytton. Seven male and two female characters. Costumes of the period of George I of England. Scenery illustrative of London localities, and residences of the same era. Time of playing, one hour and ten minutes.

92 MY WIFE'S OUT. A Farce in one act, by G. Herbert Rodwell. Two male and two female characters. This piece had a successful run at the Covent Garden Theatre, London. Costume modern, and scene an artist's studio. Time in representation, forty minutes.

93 THE AREA BELLE. A Farce in one act, by William Brough and Andrew Halliday. Three male and two female characters. Costumes of the present time, and scene a kitchen. Time in performing, thirty minutes.

94 OUR CLERKS; or, No. 3, Fig Tree Court, Temple. An original Farce, in one act. Seven male and five female characters. Costumes modern, and scene a large sitting room solidly furnished. Time in representation, sixty-five minutes.

95 THE PRETTY HORSE BREAKER. A Farce, by Wil- liam Brough and Andrew Halliday. Three male and ten female characters. Costumes modern English, and scene a breakfast room in a fashionble mausion. Time of playing, forty-five minutes.

96 DEAREST MAMMA. A Comedietta in one act, by Wal- ter Gordon. Four male and three female characters. Costume modern English, and scene a drawing room. Time in representation, one hour.

97 ORANGE BLOSSOMS. A Comedietta in one act, by J. P. Wooler. Three male and three female characters. Costume of the present day, and scene, a garden with summer house. Time in playing, fifty minutes.

98 WHO IS WHO? or, All in a Fog. A Farce, adapted from the French, by Thomas J. Williams. Three male and two female characters. Costumes, modern English dresses, as worn by country gentry ; and scene, parlor, in an old fashioned country house. Time of playing, thirty minutes.

99 THE FIFTH WHEEL. A Comedy in three acts. Ten male and two female characters. An excellent American production, easily managed. Costumes of the modern day. Scenery not complicated. Time of representation, about one hour and three quarters.

100 JACK LONG. A Drama in two acts, by J. B. John- stone. Nine male and two female characters. Costume of the frontiers. Scenery illustrative of localities on the Texan frontier. Time of performance, one hour and twenty minutes.

101 FERNANDE; or, Forgive and Forget. A Drama in three acts, by Victorien Sardou. Eleven male and ten female characters. This is a correct version of the celebrated play as performed in Paris and adapted to the English stage, by Henry L. Williams, Jr. Costumes, modern French. Scenery, four interiors. Time in representation, three hours.

102 FOILED; or, a Struggle for Life and Liberty. A Drama in four acts, by O. W. Cornish. 9 males, 3 females. Costumes, modern American. Scenery—a variety of scenes required, but none elaborate. Time in representation, three and a half hours.

No.

103 FAUST AND MARGUERITE. A romantic Drama in three acts, translated from the French of Michel Carre, by Thomas William Robertson. Nine male and seven female characters. Costumes German, of the sixteenth century; doublets, trunks, tights. Scenery, a laboratory, tavern, garden, street and tableau. Time in representation, two hours.

104 NO NAME. A Drama in five acts, by Wilkie Collins. Seven male and five female characters. A dramatization of the author's popular novel of the same name. Costumes of the present day. Scenery, four interiors and a sea view. Time in representation, three hours.

105 WHICH OF THE TWO. A Comedietta in one act, by John M. Morton. Two male and ten female characters. A very neat and interesting petty comedy. Costume Russian. Scene, public room of an Inn. Time of playing, fifty minutes.

106 UP FOR THE CATTLE SHOW. A Farce in one act, by Harry Lemon. Six male and two female characters. Costumes English, of the present day. Scene, a parlor. Time in representation, forty minutes.

107 CUPBOARD LOVE. A Farce in one act, by Frederick Hay. Two male and one female characters. A good specimen of broad comedy. Dresses modern, and scene, a neatly furnished apartment. Time in representation, twenty minutes.

108 MR. SCROGGINS; or, Change of Name. A Farce in one act, by William Hancock. Three male and three female characters. A lively piece. Costumes of the present day. Scene, a drawing room. Time in representation, forty minutes.

109 LOCKED IN. A Comedietta in one act, by J. P. Wool- er. Two male and two female characters. Costumes of the period. Scene, a drawing room. Time in representation, thirty minutes.

110 POPPLETON'S PREDICAMENTS. A Farce in one act, by Charles M. Rae. Three male and six female characters. Costumes of the day. Scene, a drawing room. Time in representation, forty minutes.

111 THE LIAR. A Comedy in two acts, by Samuel Foote. Seven male and two female characters. One of the best acting plays in any language. Costumes, embroidered court dresses, silk sacques, &c; still the modern dress will suffice. Scenes—one, a park, the other a drawing room. Time in representation, one hour and twenty minutes. This edition, as altered by Charles Mathews, is particularly adapted for amateurs.

112 NOT A BIT JEALOUS. A Farce in one act, by T. W. Robertson. Three male and three female characters. Costumes of the day. Scene, a room. Time of playing, forty minutes.

113 CYRIL'S SUCCESS. A Comedy in five acts, by Henry J. Byron. Ten male and four female characters. Costumes modern. Scenery, four interiors. Time in representation, three hours twenty minutes.

114 ANYTHING FOR A CHANGE. A petite Comedy in one act, by Shirley Brooks. Three male and three female characters. Costumes present day. Scene, an interior. Time in representation, fifty-one minutes.

115 NEW MEN AND OLD ACRES. A Comedy in three acts by Tom Taylor. Eight male and five female characters. Costumes present day. Scenery somewhat complicated. Time in representation, two hours.

116 I'M NOT MESILF AT ALL. An original Irish Stew in one act, by C. A. Maltby. Three male and two female characters. Costume of present day, undress uniform, Irish peasant and Highland dress. Scene, a room. Time in playing twenty-eight minutes.

No.

132 A RACE FOR A DINNER. A Farce in one act, by
J. F. G. Rodwell. Ten male characters. A sterling piece. Costumes of
the day. Scene, a tavern exterior. Time in representation, sixty minutes.

133 TIMOTHY TO THE RESCUE. A Farce in one act,
by Henry J. Byron. Four male and two female characters. In this
laughable piece Spangle assumes several personifications. Costumes of
the day, and scene a plain interior. Time in representation, forty-five
minutes.

134 TOMPKINS, THE TROUBADOUR. A Farce in one
act, by MM. Lockroy and Marc Michel. Three male and two female characters. Costumes modern, and scene an ironmonger's shop. Time in playing, thirty-five minutes.

135 EVERYBODY'S FRIEND. A Comedy in three acts,
by J. Sterling Coyne. Six male and five female characters. Costumes
modern, and scenery three interiors. Time in performance, two and a
half hours.

136 THE WOMAN IN RED. A Drama in three acts and
Prologue, by J. Sterling Coyne. Six male and eight female characters.
Costumes French and Italian. Scenery complicated. Time of playing,
three hours and twenty-five minutes.

137 L'ARTICLE 47; or Breaking the Ban. A Drama in
three acts, by Adolph Belot, adapted to the English stage by Henry L.
Williams. Eleven male and five female characters. Costumes French,
of the day. Scenery elaborate. Time in representation, three hours and
ten minutes.

138 POLL AND PARTNER JOE; or, The Pride of Put-
ney and the Pressing Pirate. A Burlesque in one act and four scenes, by
F. C. Burnand. Ten male and three female characters. (Many of the male
characters are performed by ladies.) Costumes modern, and scenery local.
Time of playing, one hour.

139 JOY IS DANGEROUS. A Comedy in two acts, by
James Mortimer. Three male and three female characters. Costume,
modern French. Scenery, two interiors. Time in representation, one
hour and forty-five minutes.

140 NEVER RECKON YOUR CHICKENS, &c. A Farce
in one act, by Wybert Reeve. Three male and four female characters.
Modern costumes, and scene, an interior. Time in representation, forty
minutes.

•141 THE BELLS; or, the Polish Jew. A romantic moral
Drama in three acts, by MM. Erckmann and Chatrian. Nine male and three
female characters. Costumes Alsatian. of present date. Scenery, two
interiors and a court room. Time of playing, two hours and twenty minutes.

142 DOLLARS AND CENTS. An original American Com-
edy in three acts, by L. J. Hollenius, as performed by the Murray Hill
Dramatic Association. Nine male and four female characters. Costumes
modern, and scenery, three interiors and one garden. Time in representation, two and three quarter hours.

143 LODGERS AND DODGERS. A Farce in one act, by
Frederick Hay. Four male and two female characters. Costumes of
the present time. Scene, a furnished apartment. Time in representation,
twenty-five minutes. One character a Yorkshire farmer.

144 THE LANCASHIRE LASS; or, Tempted, Tried and
True. A domestic Melodrama in four acts and a Prologue, by Henry J.
Byron. Twelve male and three female characters. Costumes of the present day. Scenery, varied and difficult. Time in representation, three
hours.

No.

158 SCHOOL. A Comedy in four acts, by T. W. Robertson. Six male and six female characters. Is a very superior piece, and has three characters unusually good for either sex. Could be played with fine effect at a girls' seminary. Costumes modern. Scenery, English landscape and genteel interiors. Time in representation, two hours and forty minutes.

159 IN THE WRONG HOUSE. A Farce in one act, by Martin Becher. Four male and two female characters. A very justly popular piece. Two of the male characters are excellent for light and low comedian. Good parts, too, for a young and old lady. Costumes modern. Scenery, an ordinary room. Time in representation, twenty-five minutes.

160 BLOW FOR BLOW. A Drama in a Prologue and three acts, by Henry J. Byron. Eleven male and six female characters. Full of homely pathos as well as rich humor. Has several excellent parts. Costumes modern. Scenery, interiors of offices and dwellings. Time in representation, three hours.

161 WOMAN'S VOWS AND MASONS' OATHS. In four acts, by A. J. H. Duganne. Ten male and four female characters. Has effective situations, fine characters and beautiful dialogues. Costumes modern, with Federal and Confederate uniforms. Scenery, interiors in country houses, and warlike encampments. Time in performance, two hours and thirty minutes.

162 UNCLE'S WILL. A Comedietta in one act, by S. Theyre Smith. Two male and one female characters. A brilliant piece; can be easily played in a parlor. Costumes modern, and naval uniform for Charles. Scenery, set interior drawing room. Time in representation, thirty minutes.

163 MARCORETTI. A romantic Drama in three acts, by John M. Kingdom. Ten male and three female characters. A thrillingly effective piece, full of strong scenes. Costumes, brigands and rich Italian's dress. Scenery, interior of castle, mountain passes, and princely ball room. Time in representation, two hours.

164 LITTLE RUBY; or, Home Jewels. A domestic Drama in three acts, by J. J. Wallace. Six male and six female characters. This drama is at once affecting and effective. Little Ruby fine personation for young prodigy. Costumes modern. Scenery, interior of dwelling and gardens. Time in representation, two hours.

165 THE LIVING STATUE. A Farce in one act, by Joseph J. Dilley and James Allen. Three male and two female characters. Brimful of fun. Trotter a great character for a droll low comedian. Costumes modern, with one old Roman warrior dress. Scenery, a plain interior.

166 BARDELL vs. PICKWICK. A Farcical sketch in one act, arranged from Charles Dickens. Six male and two female characters. Uncommonly funny. Affords good chance to 'take off" local legal celebrities. Costumes modern. Scenery, a court room. Time in performance, thirty minutes.

167 APPLE BLOSSOMS. A Comedy in three acts, by James Albery. Seven male and three female characters. A pleasing piece, with rich part for an eccentric comedian. Costumes modern English. Scenery, exterior and interior of inn. Time in representation, two hours and twenty minutes.

168 TWEEDIE'S RIGHTS. A Comedy in two acts, by James Albery. Four male and two female characters. Has several excellent characters. John Tweedie, powerful personation; Tim Whiffler very funny. Costumes modern. Scenery, a stone mason's yard and modest interior. Time in representation, one hour and twenty-five minutes.

o.

69 MY UNCLE'S SUIT. A Farce in one act, by Martin Becher. Four male and one female characters. Has a jolly good low comedy part, a fine light comedy one, and a brisk, pert lady's maid. Costumes modern. Scenery, a well furnished sitting room. Time in representation, thirty minutes.

70 ONLY SOMEBODY; or, Dreadfully Alarming. A Farce in one act, by Conway Edwardes and Edward Cullerne. Four male and two female characters. Immensely funny. Full of queer incidents. Every way fitted for amateurs. Costumes modern. Scenery, a garden and back of a house. Time of playing, thirty minutes.

71 NOTHING LIKE PASTE. A Farce in one act, by Chas. Marsham Rae. Three male and one female characters. Every character superexcellent. Billy Doo a regular Burtonian part. Admirable piece for amateurs. Costumes modern. Scenery, exterior of a small villa, with gardens. Time in representation, forty minutes.

72 OURS. A Comedy in three acts, by T. W. Robertson. Six male and three female characters. One of the best and most admired plays in our language—while a fair stock company can play it acceptably. It has several characters fit for stars. Costumes modern, with British military uniforms. Scenery, gardens, park, drawing room, and rude hut in the Crimea. Time of representation, two hours and thirty minutes.

73 OFF THE STAGE. An entirely original Comedietta in one act, by Sydney Rosenfeld. Three male and three female characters, all equally excellent. One of the sprightliest, wittiest and most amusing little plays ever written, causing almost an hour's constant merriment. Costumes modern. Scene a handsome interior.

74 HOME. A Comedy in three acts, by T. W. Robertson. Four male, three female characters. A charming piece. Needs but a small company. Every character very good. Costumes modern. Only one scene throughout the play. Time of representation, two hours.

75 CAST UPON THE WORLD. An entirely Original Drama in five acts, by Charles E. Newton. Ten male, five female characters. A remarkably effective piece. Costumes modern. Scenery somewhat elaborate, but very fine. Time of representation, two hours and thirty minutes.

76 ON BREAD AND WATER. A Musical Farce in one act, being a free adaptation from the German, by Sydney Rosenfeld. A rollicking little piece. One male and two female characters. Containing a brilliant soubrette part. Costumes modern. Scene an uncarpeted school room. Time in representation, twenty-five minutes.

77 I SHALL INVITE THE MAJOR. A Parlor Comedy in one act, by G. von Moser. Containing five characters, four male and one female. A very pleasing little play, with good parts for all. Very bright and witty. Costumes modern. Scene, a handsome interior. Time in representation, forty minutes.

78 OUT AT SEA. An entirely Original Romantic Drama in a prologue and four acts, by Charles E. Newton. Sixteen male, five female characters. Powerfully written. Full of strong situations. Very telling scenic effects. Costumes modern. Time in representation, two hours and ten minutes.

79 A BREACH OF PROMISE. An extravagant Comic Drama in two acts, by T. W. Robertson. Five male, two female characters. A capital, very merry piece. Good for amateurs. Time in representation, one hour. Scenery, two interiors. Costume, modern.

80 HENRY THE FIFTH. An Historical Play in five acts. By William Shakspeare. Thirty-eight male, five female characters. This grand play has a rare blending of the loftiest tragedy, with the richest and broadest humor. This edition is the most complete in every respect ever published. Costumes rich and expensive. Scenery, etc., very elaborate. Time of representation, three hours.

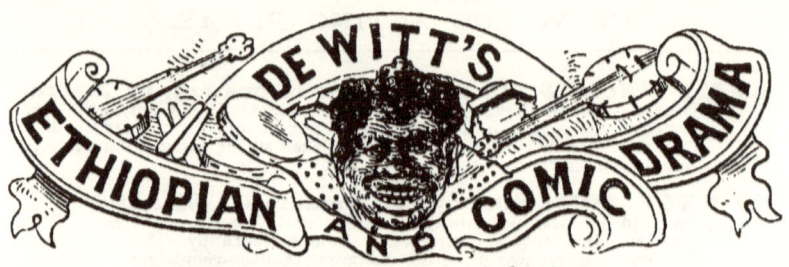

"Let those laugh now who never laughed before;
And those who always laughed now laugh the more."

Nothing so thorough and complete in the way of Ethiopian and Comic Dramas has ever been printed as those that appear in the following list. Not only are the plots excellent, the characters droll, the incidents funny, the language humorous, but all the situations, by-play, positions, pantomimic business, scenery and tricks are so plainly set down and clearly explained, that the merest novice could put any of them on the Stage. Included in this Catalogue are all the most laughable and effective pieces of their class ever produced.

*** In ordering, please copy the figures at the commencement of each Play, which indicate the number of the piece in "DE WITT'S ETHIOPIAN AND COMIC DRAMA."

☞ Any of the following Plays sent, postage free, on receipt of price—fifteen cents.

Address as on first page of this Catalogue.

DE WITT'S ETHIOPIAN 🙂 COMIC DRAMA.

No.

1 THE LAST OF THE MOHICANS. An Ethiopian Sketch, by J. C. Stewart. Three male and one female characters. Costumes of the day, except Indian shirts, &c. Two scenes, chamber and wood. Time in representation, eighteen minutes.

2 TRICKS. An Ethiopian Sketch, by J. C. Stewart. Five male and two female characters. Costumes of the period. Two scenes, two interiors. Time in representation, eighteen minutes.

3 HEMMED IN. An Ethiopian Sketch, by J. C. Stewart. Three male and one female characters. Costumes modern, and scene, a studio. Time in representation, twenty minutes.

4 EH? WHAT IS IT? An Ethiopian Sketch, by J. C. Stewart. Four male and one female characters. Costumes of the day, and scene, a chamber. Time in representation, twenty minutes.

5 TWO BLACK ROSES. An Ethiopian Sketch, by J. C. Stewart. Four male and one female characters. Costumes modern, and scene, an apartment. Time in representation, twenty minutes.

No.

6 THE BLACK CHAP FROM WHITECHAPEL. An eccentric Negro Piece, adapted from Burnand and Williams' "B. B" by Henry L. Williams, Jr. Four male characters. Costumes modern. Scene, an interior. Time in representation, thirty minutes.

7 THE STUPID SERVANT. An Ethiopian Sketch in one scene, by Charles White. Two male characters. Characters very droll; fit for star "darky" players. Costumes modern and fantastic dresses. Scenery, an ordinary room. Time in representation, twenty minutes.

8 THE MUTTON TRIAL. An Ethiopian Sketch in two scenes, by James Maffit. Four male characters. Capital burlesque of courts of "justice;" all the parts good. Costumes modern and Quaker. Scenery, a wood view and a court room. Time in representation, twenty minutes.

9 THE POLICY PLAYERS. An Ethiopian Sketch in one scene, by Charles White. Seven male characters. A very clever satire upon a sad vice. Costumes modern, and coarse negro ragged clothes. Scenery, an ordinary kitchen. Time in representation, twenty minutes.

10 THE BLACK CHEMIST. An Ethiopian Sketch in one scene, by Charles White. Three male characters. All the characters are A 1, funny in the extreme. Costumes modern or Yankee—extravagant. Scenery, an apothecary's laboratory. Time in representation, seventeen minutes.

11 BLACK-EY'D WILLIAM. An Ethiopian Sketch in two scenes, by Charles White. Four male, one female characters. All the parts remarkably good. Costumes as extravagant as possible. Scenery, a police court room. Time in representation, twenty minutes.

12 DAGUERREOTYPES. An Ethiopian Sketch in one scene, by Charles White. Three male characters. Full of broad humor; all characters excellent. Costumes modern genteel, negro and Yankee garbs. Scenery, ordinary room with camera. Time in representation, fifteen minutes.

13 THE STREETS OF NEW YORK; or, **New York by** Gaslight. An Ethiopian Sketch in one scene, by Charles White. Six male characters. Three of the parts very droll; others good. Costumes some modern, some Yankee and some loaferish. Scenery, street view. Time in representation, eighteen minutes.

14 THE RECRUITING OFFICE. An Ethiopian Sketch in one act, by Charles White. Five male characters. A piece full of incidents to raise mirth. Three of the parts capital. Costumes extravagant, white and darkey, and a comical uniform. Scenery, plain chamber and a street. Time in representation, fifteen minutes.

15 SAM'S COURTSHIP. An Ethiopian Farce in one act, by Charles White. Two male and one female characters. All the characters particularly jolly. Two of the parts can be played in either white or black, and one in Dutch. Costumes Yankee and modern. Scenery, plain chamber. Time in representation, twenty minutes.

16 STORMING THE FORT. A burlesque Ethiopian Sketch in one scene, by Charles White. Five male characters. Richly ludicrous; all the characters funny. Costumes fantastical, and extravagant military uniforms. Scenery, ludicrous "take off" of fortifications. Time in representation, fifteen minutes.

17 THE GHOST. An Ethiopian Sketch in one act, by Charles White. Two male characters. A right smart piece, full of laugh. Costumes ordinary "darkey" clothes. Scenery common looking kitchen. Time in representation, fifteen minutes.

18 THE LIVE INDIAN; or, **Jim Crow.** A comical Ethiopian Sketch in four scenes, by Dan Bryant. Four male, one female characters. As full of fun as a hedgehog is full of bristles. Costumes modern and darkey. Scenery, chamber and street. Time in representation, twenty minutes.

No.

19 MALICIOUS TRESPASS; or, Points of Law. An Ethi-opian Sketch in one scene, by Charles White. Three male characters. Extravagantly comical; all the parts very good. Costumes extravagant modern garbs. Scenery, wood or landscape. Time of playing, twenty minutes.

20 GOING FOR THE CUP; or, Old Mrs. Williams' Dance. An Ethiopian Interlude, by Charles White. Four male characters. One capital part for a bright juvenile; the others very droll. Costumes modern and darkey. Scenery, a landscape or wood. Time in representation, twenty minutes.

21 SCAMPINI. An anti-tragical, comical, magical and laughable Pantomime, full of tricks and transformations, in two scenes, by Edward Warden. Six male, three female characters. Costumes extravagantly eccentric. Scenery, plain rustic chamber. Time in representation, thirty minutes.

22 OBEYING ORDERS. An Ethiopian Military Sketch in one scene, by John Arnold. Two male, one female characters. Mary Jane, a capital wench part. The piece very jocose. Costumes ludicrous military and old style dresses. Scenery either plain or fancy chamber. Time of playing, fifteen minutes.

23 HARD TIMES. A Negro Extravaganza in one scene, by Daniel D. Emmett. Five male, one female characters. Needs several good players—then there is "music in the air." Costumes burlesque, fashionable and low negro dresses. Scenery, a kitchen. Time in representation, twenty minutes.

24 BRUISED AND CURED. A Negro Burlesque Sketch in one scene, by A. J. Leavitt. Two male characters. A rich satire upon the muscular furore of the day. Costumes tights and guernsey shirts and negro dress. Scenery, plain chamber. Time in representation, twenty minutes.

25 THE FELLOW THAT LOOKS LIKE ME. A laughable Interlude in one scene, by Oliver Durivarge. Two male characters—one female. Boiling over with fun, especially if one can make up like Lester Wallack. Costumes genteel modern. Scenery, handsome chamber. Time in representation, twenty-five minutes.

26 RIVAL TENANTS. A Negro Sketch, by George L. Stout. Four male characters. Humorously satirical; the parts all very funny. Costumes negro and modern. Scenery, an old kitchen. Time of playing, twenty minutes.

27 ONE HUNDREDTH NIGHT OF HAMLET. A Negro Sketch, by Charles White. Seven male, one female characters. Affords excellent chance for imitations of popular "stars." Costumes modern, some very shabby. Scenery, plain chamber. Time in representation, twenty minutes.

28 UNCLE EPH'S DREAM. An Original Negro Sketch in two scenes and two tableaux, arranged by Charles White. Three male, one female characters. A very pathetic little piece, with a sprinkling of humor. Costumes, a modern southern dress and negro toggery. Scenery, wood, mansion and negro hut. Time in representation, twenty minutes.

29 WHO DIED FIRST? A Negro Sketch in one Scene, by A. J. Leavitt. Three male, one female characters. Jasper and Hannah are both very comical personages. Costumes, ordinary street dress and common darkey clothes. Scenery, a kitchen. Time in representation, twenty minutes.

30 ONE NIGHT IN A BAR ROOM. A Burlesque Sketch, arranged by Charles White. Seven male characters. Has a funny Dutchman and two good darkey characters. Costume, one Dutch and several modern. Scenery, an ordinary interior. Time in representation, twenty minutes.

No.

31 GLYCERINE OIL. An Ethiopian Sketch, by John Arnold. Three male characters, all good. Costumes, Quaker and eccentric modern. Scenery, a street and a kitchen. Time in representation, fifteen minutes.

32 WAKE UP, WILLIAM HENRY. A Negro Sketch, arranged by Charles White. Three male characters, which have been favorites of our best performers. Costumes modern—some eccentric. Scenery plain chamber. Time in representation, ten minutes.

33 JEALOUS HUSBAND. A Negro Sketch, arranged by Charles White. Two male, one female characters. Full of farcical dialogue. Costumes, ordinary modern dress. Scenery, a fancy rustic chamber. Time in representation, twenty minutes.

34 THREE STRINGS TO ONE BOW. An Ethiopian Sketch in one scene, arranged by Charles White. Four male, one female characters. Full of rough, practical jokes. Costumes, modern. Scenery, a landscape. Time in representation, fifteen minutes.

35 COAL HEAVERS' REVENGE. A Negro Sketch in one scene, by George L. Stout. Six male characters. The two coal heavers have "roaring" parts. Costumes, modern, Irish and negro comic make up. Scenery, landscape. Time in representation, twenty minutes.

36 LAUGHING GAS. A Negro Burlesque Sketch in one scene, arranged by Charles White. Six male, one female characters. Is a favorite with our best companies. Costumes, one modern genteel, the rest ordinary negro. Scenery, plain chamber. Time of playing, fifteen minutes.

37 A LUCKY JOB. A Negro Farce in two scenes, arranged by Charles White. Three male, two female characters. A rattling, lively piece. Costumes, modern and eccentric. Scenery, street and fancy chamber. Time in representation, thirty minutes.

38 SIAMESE TWINS. A Negro Burlesque Sketch, in two scenes, arranged by Charles White. Five male characters. One of the richest in fun of any going. Costumes, Irish, darkey and one wizard's dress. Scenery, a street and a chamber. Time in representation, twenty-five minutes.

39 WANTED A NURSE. A laughable Sketch in one scene, arranged by Charles White. Four male characters. All the characters first rate. Costume, modern, extravagant, one Dutch dress. Scenery, a plain kitchen. Time in representation, twenty minutes.

40 A BIG MISTAKE. A Negro Sketch in one scene, by A. J. Leavitt. Four male characters. Full of most absurdly funny incidents. Costumes, modern; one policeman's uniform. Scenery, a plain chamber. Time in representation, eighteen minutes.

41. CREMATION. An Ethiopian Sketch in two scenes, by A. J. Leavitt. Eight male, one female characters. Full of broad, palpable hits at the last sensation. Costumes modern, some eccentric. Scenery, a street and a plain chamber. Time in representation, twenty-five minutes.

42. BAD WHISKEY. A comic Irish Sketch in one scene, by Sam Rickey and Master Borney. Two male, one female characters. One of the very best of its class. Extravagant low Irish dress and a policeman's uniform.

43 BABY ELEPHANT. A Negro Sketch in two scenes. By J. C. Stewart. Seven male, one female characters. Uproariously comic in idea and execution. Costumes, modern. Scenery, one street, one chamber. Time in representation, twenty-five minutes.

44 THE MUSICAL SERVANT. An Ethiopian Sketch in one scene, by Phil. H. Mowrey. Three male characters. Very original and very droll. Costumes, modern and low darkey. Scenery, a plain chamber. Time in representation, fifteen minutes.

No.

58 GHOST IN A PAWN SHOP. An Ethiopian Sketch in
one scene, by Mr. Mackey. Four male characters. As comical as its title ;
running over with practical jokes. Time of representation, twenty minutes.

59 THE SAUSAGE MAKERS. A Negro Burlesque Sketch
in two scenes, arranged by Charles White. Five male, one female characters. An old story worked up with a deal of laughable effect. The ponder-
ous sausage machine and other properties need not cost more than a
couple of dollars. Time of representation, twenty minutes.

60 THE LOST WILL. A Negro Sketch, by A. J. Leavitt.
Four male characters. Very droll from the word "go." Time of representation, eighteen minutes.

61 THE HAPPY COUPLE. A Short Humorous scene, ar-
ranged by Charles White. Two male, one female characters. A spirited
burlesque of foolish jealousy. Sam is a very frolicsome, and very funny
young darkey. Time of playing, seventeen minutes.

62 VINEGAR BITTERS. A Negro Sketch in one scene, ar-
ranged by Charles White. Six male, one female characters. A broad burlesque of the popular patent medicine business ; plenty of humorous incidents. Time of representation, fifteen minutes.

63 THE DARKEY'S STRATAGEM. A Negro Sketch in one
act, arranged by Charles White. Three male, one female characters. Quaint
courtship scenes of a pair of young darkies, ludicrously exaggerated by the
tricks of the boy Cupid. Time of representation, twenty minutes.

64 THE DUTCHMAN'S GHOST. In one scene, by Larry
Tooley. Four male, one female characters. Jacob Schrochorn, the jolly
shoemaker and his frau, are rare ones for raising a hearty laugh. Time of
representation, fifteen minutes.

65 PORTER'S TROUBLES. An Amusing Sketch in one
scene, by Ed. Harrigan. Six male, one female characters. A laughable ex-
position of the queer freaks of a couple of eccentric lodgers that pester a
poor "porter." Time in representation, eighteen minutes.

66 PORT WINE vs. JEALOUSY. A Highly Amusing
Sketch, by William Carter. Two male, one female characters. Twenty
minutes jammed full of the funniest kind of fun.

67 EDITOR'S TROUBLES. A Farce in one scene, by Ed-
ward Harrigan. Six male characters. A broad farcical description of the
running of a country journal "under difficulties." Time of representation, twenty-three minutes.

68 HIPPOTHEATRON OR BURLESQUE CIRCUS. An
Extravagant, funny Sketch, by Charles White. Nine male characters. A
rich burlesque of sports in the ring and stone smashing prodigies. Time of
playing, varies with "acts" introduced.

69 SQUIRE FOR A DAY. A Negro Sketch, by A. J.
Leavitt. Five male, one female characters. The "humor of it" is in the
mock judicial antics of a darkey judge for a day. Time of representation,
twenty minutes.

70 GUIDE TO THE STAGE. An Ethiopian Sketch, by Chas.
White. Three male characters. Contains some thumping theatrical hits of
the "Lay on Macduff," style. Time of playing, twelve minutes.

MANUSCRIPT PLAYS,

Below will be found a List of nearly all the great Dramatic successes of the present and past seasons. Every one of these Plays, it will be noticed, are the productions of the most eminent Dramatists of the age. Nothing is omitted that can in any manner lighten the duties of the Stage Manager, the Scene Painter or the Property Man.

ON THE JURY. A Drama, in four Acts. By Watts Phil-lips. This piece has seven male and four female characters.

ELFIE; or, THE CHERRY TREE INN. A Romantic Drama, in three Acts. By Dion Boucicault. This piece has six male and four female characters.

THE TWO THORNS. A Comedy, in four Acts. By James Albery. This piece has nine male and three female characters.

A WRONG MAN IN THE RIGHT PLACE. A Farce, in one Act. By John Oxenford. This piece has one male and three female characters.

JEZEBEL; or, THE DEAD RECKONING. By Dion Bou-cicault. This piece has six male and five female characters.

THE RAPAREE; or, THE TREATY OF LIMERICK. A Drama, in three Acts. By Dion Boucicault. This piece has nine male and two female characters.

'TWIXT AXE AND CROWN; or, THE LADY ELIZA-beth. An Historical Play, in five Acts. By Tom Taylor. This piece has twenty-five male and twelve female characters.

THE TWO ROSES. A Comedy, in three Acts. By James Albery. This piece has five male and four female characters.

M. P. (Member of Parliament.) A Comedy, in four Acts. By T. W. Robertson. This piece has seven male and five female characters.

MARY WARNER. A Domestic Drama, in four Acts. By Tom Taylor. This piece has eleven male and five female characters.

PHILOMEL. A Romantic Drama, in three Acts. By H. T. Craven. This piece has six male and four female characters.

UNCLE DICK'S DARLING. A Domestic Drama, in three Acts. By Henry J. Byron. This piece has six male and five female characters.

LITTLE EM'LY. (David Copperfield.) A Drama, in four Acts. By Andrew Halliday. "Little Em'ly" has eight male and eight female characters.

FORMOSA. A Drama, in four Acts. By Dion Boucicault.
This piece has eighteen male and eight female characters.

HOME. A Comedy, in three Acts. By T. W. Robertson.
"Home" has four male and three female characters.

AN ENGLISH GENTLEMAN; or, THE SQUIRE'S LAST
Shilling. A Drama, in four Acts. By Henry J. Byron. This piece contains nine male, four female characters.

FOUL PLAY. A Drama, in four Acts. By Dion Boucicault.
This piece has fourteen male and two female characters.

AFTER DARK. A Drama, in four Acts. By Dion Boucicault. This piece has fourteen male and two female characters.

ARRAH-NA-POGUE. A Drama, in three Acts. By Dion
Boucicault. This piece has fourteen male and two female characters.

BREACH OF PROMISE. A Comic Drama, in two Acts. By
T. W. Robertson. The piece has five male and two female characters.

BLACK AND WHITE. A Drama, in three Acts. By Wilkie
Collins and Charles Fechter. This piece has six male and two female characters.

PARTNERS FOR LIFE. A Comedy, in three Acts. By
Henry J. Byron. This piece has seven male and four female characters.

KERRY; or, Night and Morning. A Comedy, in one Act.
By Dion Boucicault. This piece contains four male and two female characters.

HINKO; or, THE HEADSMAN'S DAUGHTER. A Romantic Play, in a Prologue and five Acts. By W. G. Wills. The Prologue contains four male and three female characters. The Play contains ten male and seven female characters.

NOT IF I KNOW IT. A Farce, in one Act. By John Maddison Morton. This piece contains four male and four female characters.

DAISY FARM. A Drama, in four Acts. By Henry J. Byron
This piece contains ten male and four female characters.

EILEEN OGE; or, DARK'S THE HOUR BEFORE THE
Dawn. A Drama, in four Acts. By Edmund Falconer. This piece contains fifteen male and four female characters.

TWEEDIE'S RIGHTS. A Comedy-Drama, in two Acts. By
James Albery. This piece has four male, two female characters.

NOTRE DAME; or, THE GIPSY GIRL OF PARIS. A
Romantic Drama, in three Acts. By Andrew Halliday. This play has seven male, four female characters.

JOAN OF ARC. A Tragedy, in Five Acts. By Tom Taylor.
This piece has twenty-one male, four female characters.

☞ Manuscript copies of these very effective and very successful plays are now ready, and will be furnished to Managers on very reasonable terms.

DE WITT'S ELOCUTIONARY SERIES,

PRICE 15 CENTS EACH.

*Young people who were desirous of acquiring a practical knowledge of the beauti-
ful, as well as highly useful art of Reading and Speaking correctly and elegantly,
have found great difficulty in procuring books that would teach them rather in the
manner of a genial* FRIEND *than an imperious* MASTER. *Such books we here present
to the public in "De Witt's Elocutionary Series." Not only are the selections made
very carefully from the abundant harvest of dramatic literature, but the accompany-
ing* INSTRUCTIONS *are so* PLAIN, DIRECT *and* FORCIBLE, *that the least intelligent can
easily understand all the rules and precepts of the glorious art that has immortalized
Roscius and Kean, Chatham and Henry.*

No. 1. THE ACADEMIC SPEAKER. Containing an un-
usual variety of striking Dramatic Dialogues, and other most effective
scenes. Selected with great care and judgment from the noblest and
wittiest Dramas, Comedies and Farces most popular upon the best stages.
Interspersed with such able, plain and practical criticisms and remarks
upon Elocution and stage effects, as to render this work the most valuable
hand-book to the young orator that has ever been produced.

CONTENTS.—General Introductory Remarks ; On the quality of Selections ; On True Eloquence ;
On Awkward Delivery ; On Necessity of Attentive Study ; On Appropriate Gesture ; On the
Appearance of Ladies upon the Stage ; The Stage and the Curtain ; Remarks upon the subject
of Scenery ; How to easily Construct a Stage ; Stage Arrangements and Properties ; Remarks
upon Improvising Wardrobes, etc., etc. There are *Twelve* pieces in this book that require *two*
Male Characters ; *Six* pieces that require *six* Male Characters ; *Two* pieces that require *four*
Male Characters.

No. 2. THE DRAMATIC SPEAKER. Composed of many
very carefully chosen Monologues, Dialogues and other effective Scenes,
from the most famous Tragedies, Comedies and Farces. Interspersed with
numerous Directions and Instructions for their proper Delivery and Performance.

CONTENTS.—There are *three* pieces in this book that require *one* Male Character; *One* that requires
three Male Characters ; *Ten* that require *two* Male Characters , *Nine* that require *one* Male and
one Female Characters ; *Four* that require *three* Male Characters ; *One* that requires *two* Male and
one Female Characters ; *One* that requires *two* Female Characters ; *One* that requires *one* Male and
two Female Characters.

No. 3. THE HISTRIONIC SPEAKER. Being a careful
compilation of the most amusing Dramatic Scenes, light, gay, pointed,
witty and sparkling. Selected from the most elegantly written and most
theatrically effective Comedies and Farces upon the English and American
Stages. Properly arranged and adapted for Amateur and Parlor Representation.

CONTENTS.— *Three* of the pieces in this book require *two* Female Characters ; *One* piece requires
seven Female Characters ; *Nineteen* pieces that require *one* Male and *one* Female Characters ; *One*
piece that requires *one* Male and *two* Female Characters ; *One* piece that requires *two* Male and
one Female Characters.

No. 4. THE THESPIAN SPEAKER. Being the best Scenes
from the best Plays. Every extract is preceded by valuable and very plain
observations, teaching the young Forensic Student how to Speak and Act
in the most highly approved manner.

CONTENTS.—*Five* of the pieces in this book require *one* Male and *one* Female Characters ; *Three* of
the pieces require *three* Male Characters ; *Three* of the pieces require *two* Male and *one* Female
Characters ; *Seven* of the pieces require *two* Male Characters ; *One* of the pieces require *one* Male
and *one* Female Characters ; *Two* of the pieces require *two* Male and *two* Female Characters ; *One*
of the pieces require *four* Male and *four* Female Characters ; *Three* of the pieces require *three*
Male and *one* Female Characters.

** Single copies sent, on receipt of price, postage free.

☞ Address as per first page of this Catalogue.

OPERATIC SONGS.

COMIC AND SERIO COMIC SONGS.

MOTTO SONGS.

www.ingramcontent.com/pod-product-compliance
Lightning Source LLC
Chambersburg PA
CBHW022012050726
47499CB00007BA/2549